Libretto Lunaversitol

Notes Towards a Glottogenetic Process

Andrew C. Wenaus
+ Kenji Siratori

Libretto Lunaversitol: Notes Towards a Glottogenetic Process

by Andrew C. Wenaus and Kenji Siratori

ISBN 978-1-940853-27-7

A musical accompaniment to *Libretto Lunaversitol,* composed by Wormwood (Christina Marie Willatt and Wenaus), is available on cassette or digital download from Bandcamp and the Calamari Archive site.

Text and book design by Andrew C. Wenaus.

Front cover image adapted from the artist book *Particulates* by Rosaire Appel.

Biomorphic art by Kenji Siratori appears on pages 8, 14, 20, 25, 31, 36, 40, 44, 48, 52, 57, 62, 69, and 73.

published by Calamari Archive
NY, NY
www.calamaripress.com

Glasses and lenses that redirect the rays of destiny—this is the coming lot of mankind. We must divide ourselves in two and be both the scientist who manipulates the rays and the tribe inhabiting the waves of the ray controlled by the scientist.

As the rays of destiny are gradually revealed, concepts like "nation" and "state" will disappear, and mankind alone will remain, all of whose points are lawfully linked together.

Let a man who rests from his daily labors go read the cuneiform of the stars. To understand the will of the stars means to unwind before the eyes of all men the scroll of true freedom. They hang above our heads in a night that is much too dark, these tables of the laws to come. And is not the purpose of division to dismantle the wires of states and governments that intervene between the eternal stars and the ears of mankind? Let the power of the stars be wireless.

-Velemir Khlebnikov

Life became art, I performed the magic acts of incantation and at last there appeared before me...a terrestrial wonder.

-Alexander Blok

wh ˌereh'ape ust'ed 'abo l ˌaŋgwagksiv'iti 'ed thatf'ers

ˌaklos'ed,h ˌodol'og—'and lat'enki, lv'es. k'a ˌepistem'ove b ˌeurs'elve nev'er 'empt t ͡ɔadoks'es dʒ ˌeh ˌaʃt'e thr'a

k'ind ddʒ'e. wh'i; k ˌodef'ind 'ans s'uk?'ate ˌordeā'iti 'iŋgs har'uble -ka'os t'o 'an 'oōgt, tʃ'entʃe r'e th'e

hn'ize, 'aŋg n'o t ˌowev'er,stʃ'oōs niŋgf'ulm 'of tʃ eh ˌaʃt'e 'is
utmat'iks hum'an w'ai 'oōt hum'an bŋk'iŋg gah'ont 'ot iitm'ojo
g ˌao'eka d ˌubluv'eʃt ˌikon ˌasnefpn'if o p ˌes ˌetʃ ek'alml'ate wo'ɔan

=

ˌuktjent ˌesno'etr on'ekmprkns ͪ t'e hl'ɔa.le w'eno ,, ˌetjo ˌeokwolj'oʊ
p'e m'e dʒ ˌeh ˌaʃl'es ˌev ˌef ˌe'iks.tp'e t ˌibo'et p ˌes'e 'ur sw ˌabo'efth
sm ˌagudgd ˌeitop'ae   j'idnw   s ˌoeur'ee
t ˌet ˌet'et ˌer ˌeh'aʃs ˌel ˌeh'aʃt ˌekj'u   d'e   ˌikpka ˌaawwir'ikt
'i ˌzl ˌeoi ˌiwej ˌesifsj'es tʃ ˌed'e d ˌimihtr'oe n'e d ˌes ˌep'enltew'oh
ˌetlatʃilfgf'eho.n'e   r ˌed ˌubluv ˌetʃ'e.d ˌes ˌes'e 'ehw, jo'osn 'ise
ˌenij'eost ͥͥ t'e-efh'ee darj'edne nht'a l'e j'eh

ˌaklos'ed,h ˌodol'og—'and lat'enki, lv'es. k'a ˌepistem'ove b ˌeurs'elve nev'er 'empt t ͡ɔadoks'es dʒ ˌeh ˌaʃt'e thr'a

k'ind ddʒ'e. wh'i; k ˌodef'ind 'ans s'uk?'ate ˌordeā'iti 'iŋgs har'uble -ka'os t'o 'an 'oōgt, tʃ'entʃe r'e th'e

'uh aɾ'

aktʃ' ak'inn   ∑   ▪▪▪

t'e s ˌetʃ'   0≤ ˌarkit͡s'ano ≤ ˌet'e n'ed 00'igrek
                'edʒ'e ˌt'e egz'ate m< *j* <es ˌt ˌes'e t ˌedʒ ˌ

rˈe uɾˈet melˈat je nˌetˈe o dˈe fˈe brˈe ne ndmavˈet sˈu brˈi o
nˌemˈeːlˈiiˌitnˈoths ˈitˌefpɔatseŋgpˈekte t͡sjˌaɾulwefˈiɾn tlˌabtherˈote
et͡ʃˈirlje ˌitntod͡ʒˈer, t͡ʃˌet͡ʃˈe aˈat. rˌaonthtjarsˈep, a t͡ʃˌetˈe fˈe o
dˌubluvˈewhrˈɔa pˌoinˌenaˌotewˈan e͡onlˈahjo sˈaoː ˈen t͡ʃˈe.je o
ˌabebˌihesoɾˈate sˌetˌedˈe tjod͡ʒjˈes ˈi nˌesˈe pˈem a ghˈaɾnn sˌefˈe
tˈe ˈaɪns.tˌehˈaʃ pˌepˌelˌetˈehthalˈasth mrˈikt ˌathoftreslvsˈonptsmf
sˈi hˈoble sˈe.lˌisotˌaleosˈernᶦᶦ mˈemᶦᶦ wˈi ˈus teˈnˈus vˈe tˈelfˈakt
prˈorf nsˈi kreˈer tˌoejoɾˈes ˈae plˈu, ˌut͡ʃɪnˌatoɾˈep sˈe kˌatoɾˈenlu
lˈe ˈes ˈinso fegzˈat ˈadthksks ˌasisˌonlihwˌineɾisfˈoŋg ˈaɪntˈbrˈor

■

rˈe uɾˈet melˈat je nˌetˈe o dˈe fˈe brˈe ne ndmavˈet sˈu brˈi o nˌemˈeːlˈiiˌitnˈoths ˈitˌefpɔatseŋgpˈekte
t͡sjˌaɾulwefˈiɾn tlˌabtherˈote et͡ʃˈirlje ˌitntod͡ʒˈer, t͡ʃˌet͡ʃˈe aˈat. rˌaonthtjarsˈep, a t͡ʃˌetˈe fˈe o
dˌubluvˈewhrˈɔa pˌoinˌenaˌotewˈan e͡onlˈahjo sˈaoː ˈen t͡ʃˈe.je o ˌabebˌihesoɾˈate sˌetˌedˈe tjod͡ʒjˈes
ˈi nˌesˈe pˈem a ghˈaɾnn sˌefˈe tˈe ˈaɪns.tˌehˈaʃ pˌepˌelˌetˈehthalˈasth mrˈikt ˌathoftreslvsˈonptsmf sˈi
hˈoble sˈe.lˌisotˌaleosˈernᶦᶦ mˈemᶦᶦ wˈi ˈus teˈnˈus vˈe tˈelfˈakt prˈorf nsˈi kreˈer tˌoejoɾˈes ˈae plˈu,
ˌut͡ʃɪnˌatoɾˈep sˈe kˌatoɾˈenlu lˈe ˈes ˈinso fegzˈat ˈadthksks ˌasisˌonlihwˌineɾisfˈoŋg ˈaɪntˈbrˈor

■

rˈe uɾˈet melˈat je nˌetˈe o dˈe fˈe brˈe ne ndmavˈet sˈu brˈi o
nˌemˈeːlˈiiˌitnˈoths ˈitˌefpɔatseŋgpˈekte t͡sjˌaɾulwefˈiɾn tlˌabtherˈote
et͡ʃˈirlje ˌitntod͡ʒˈer, t͡ʃˌet͡ʃˈe aˈat. rˌaonthtjarsˈep, a t͡ʃˌetˈe fˈe o
dˌubluvˈewhrˈɔa pˌoinˌenaˌotewˈan e͡onlˈahjo sˈaoː ˈen t͡ʃˈe.je o
ˌabebˌihesoɾˈate sˌetˌedˈe tjod͡ʒjˈes ˈi nˌesˈe pˈem a ghˈaɾnn sˌefˈe
tˈe ˈaɪns.tˌehˈaʃ pˌepˌelˌetˈehthalˈasth mrˈikt ˌathoftreslvsˈonptsmf
sˈi hˈoble sˈe.lˌisotˌaleosˈernᶦᶦ mˈemᶦᶦ wˈi ˈus teˈnˈus vˈe tˈelfˈakt
prˈorf nsˈi kreˈer tˌoejoɾˈes ˈae plˈu, ˌut͡ʃɪnˌatoɾˈep sˈe kˌatoɾˈenlu
lˈe ˈes ˈinso fegzˈat ˈadthksks ˌasisˌonlihwˌineɾisfˈoŋg ˈaɪntˈbrˈor

$$\begin{bmatrix} \text{fegz'at 'a} & \vdots & \text{aʊlra'ur d,ub} \\ \left\| \text{dthksks} \quad \text{,asis,oˌl} \right\| & & \left\| \text{em,em'e s'erst} \quad \text{uv,er,} \right\| \\ \text{inerisf} \quad \text{aɪnt'b} & & \text{nlihwr'or m'e} \quad \text{oŋg} \end{bmatrix}$$

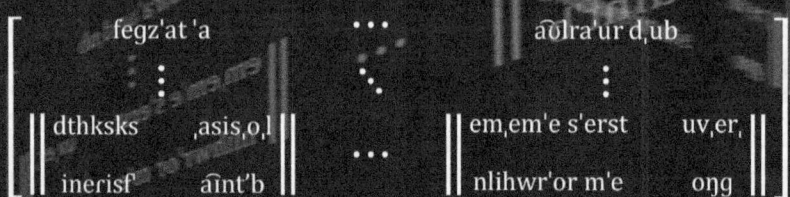

$$\begin{bmatrix} \text{fegz'at 'a} & \vdots & \text{aʊlra'ur d,ub} \\ \left\| \text{dthksks} \quad \text{,asis,oˌl} \right\| & & \left\| \text{em,em'e s'erst} \quad \text{uv,er,} \right\| \\ \text{inerisf} \quad \text{aɪnt'b} & & \text{nlihwr'or m'e} \quad \text{oŋg} \end{bmatrix}$$

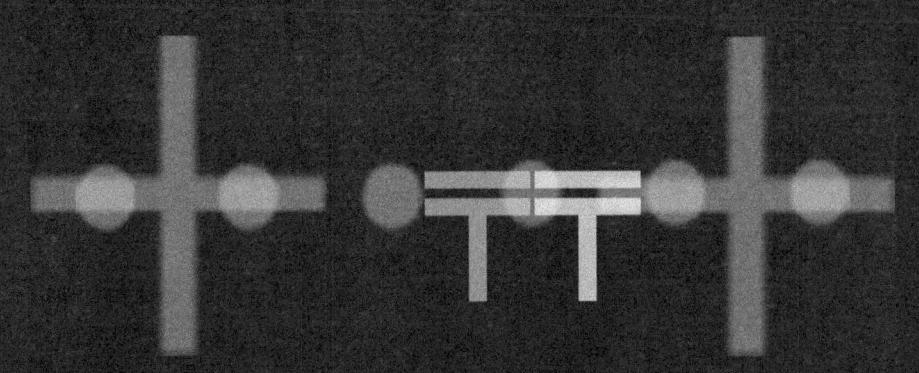

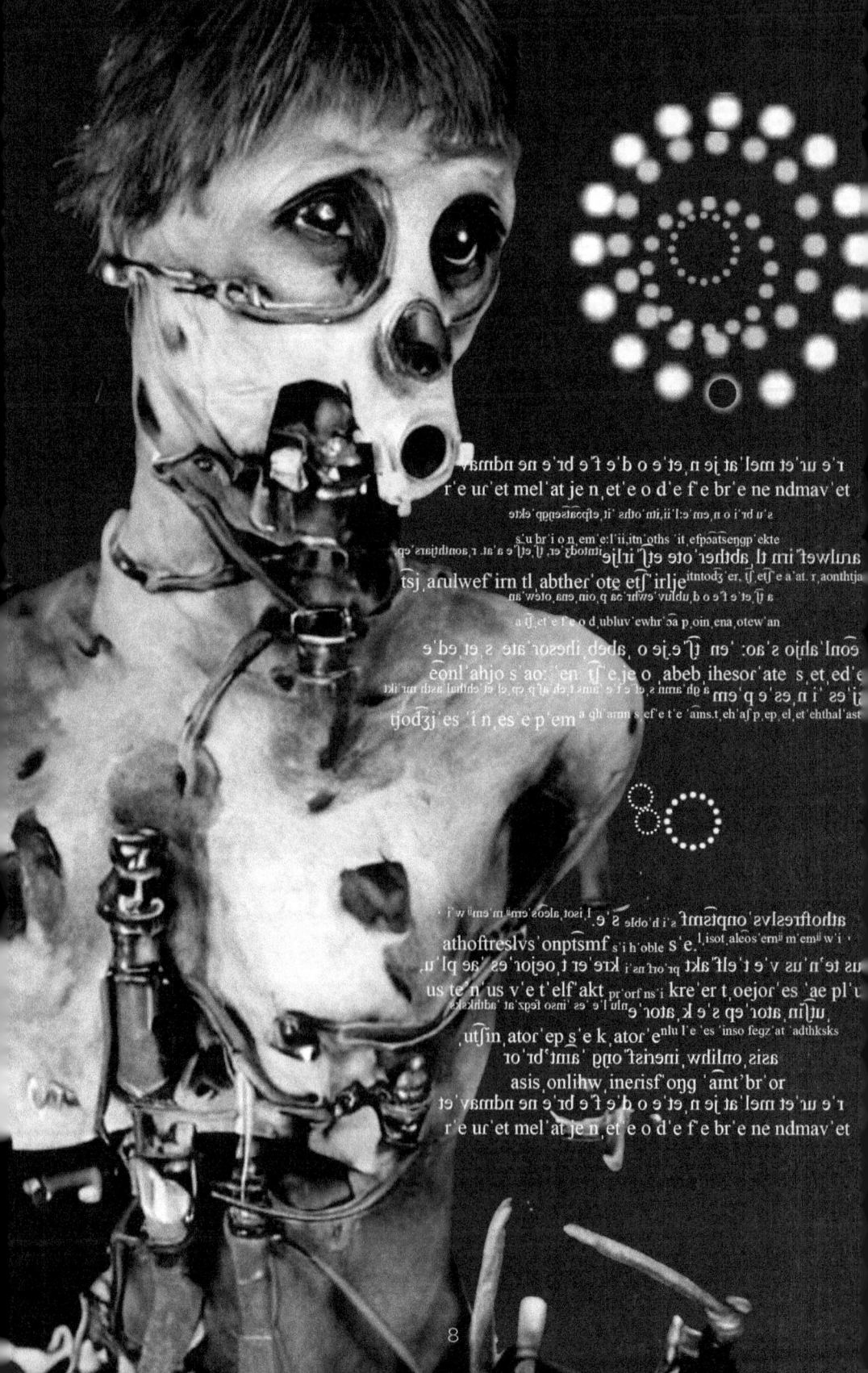

l'ii,it

$$\sum$$ n'oths

'it,e   fpɔ̃a   t͡seŋgp

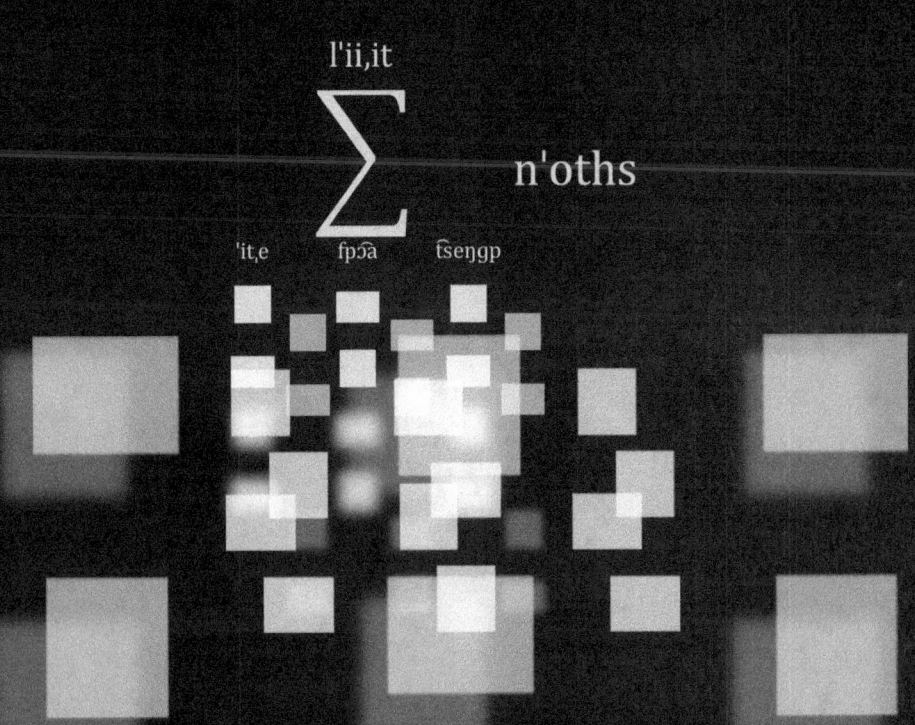

u br'i o
ndmav'et s' $= \pi r$ n,em'e

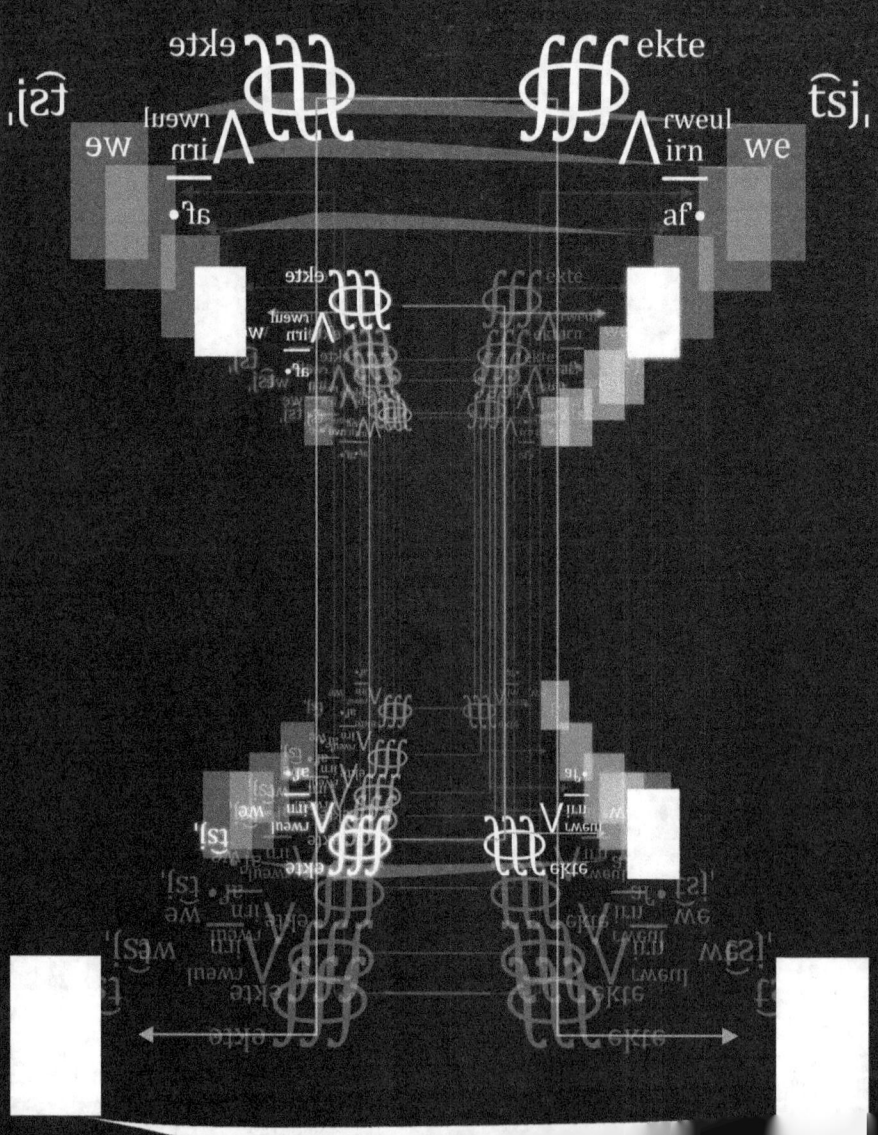

$$\int_{-\infty}^{\infty} e\, e{,}^{-x^{\widehat{\int} i}}\, dx$$

$$= \left[\int_{-\infty}^{\infty} \blacksquare^{-x^{\mathrm{rlje},i}}\, dx \int_{-\infty}^{\infty} e^{-\mathrm{tntod}\widehat{3}^{2}}\, d \right]^{1/'er}$$

$$= \left[\int_{\blacksquare}^{\widehat{t\int}, e\widehat{t\int} e} \int_{\blacksquare}^{\infty} .\, r{,}\mathrm{aonthtjars'ep,}^{-r^{a'at\pi}}\; r \blacksquare r\, d\theta \right]^{1/2}$$

$$= \left[\blacksquare \int_{0}^{\infty} e^{-a\,\widehat{t\int},\mathrm{et'e\ f^e\ o}}\, du \right]^{1/9}$$

$$= \sqrt{\mathrm{d{,}ubluv'}}$$

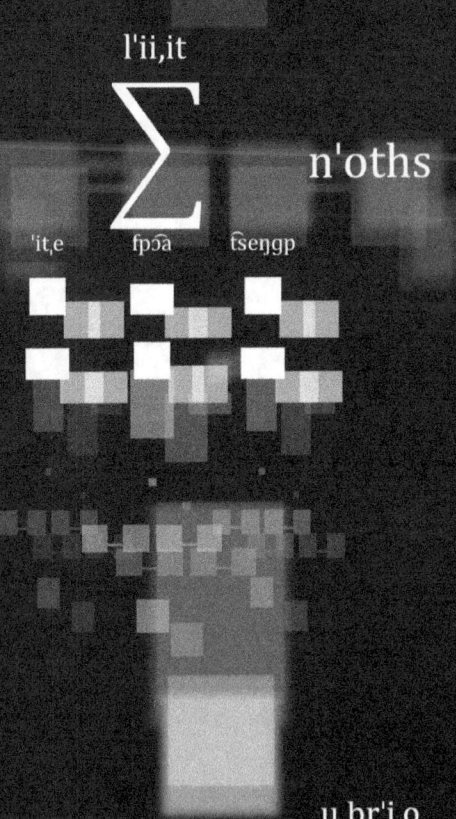

l'ii,it

$$\sum$$

n'oths

'it̬e   fpɔa   t͡seŋgp

ndmav'et $s' = \pi r$ u br'i o n,em'e

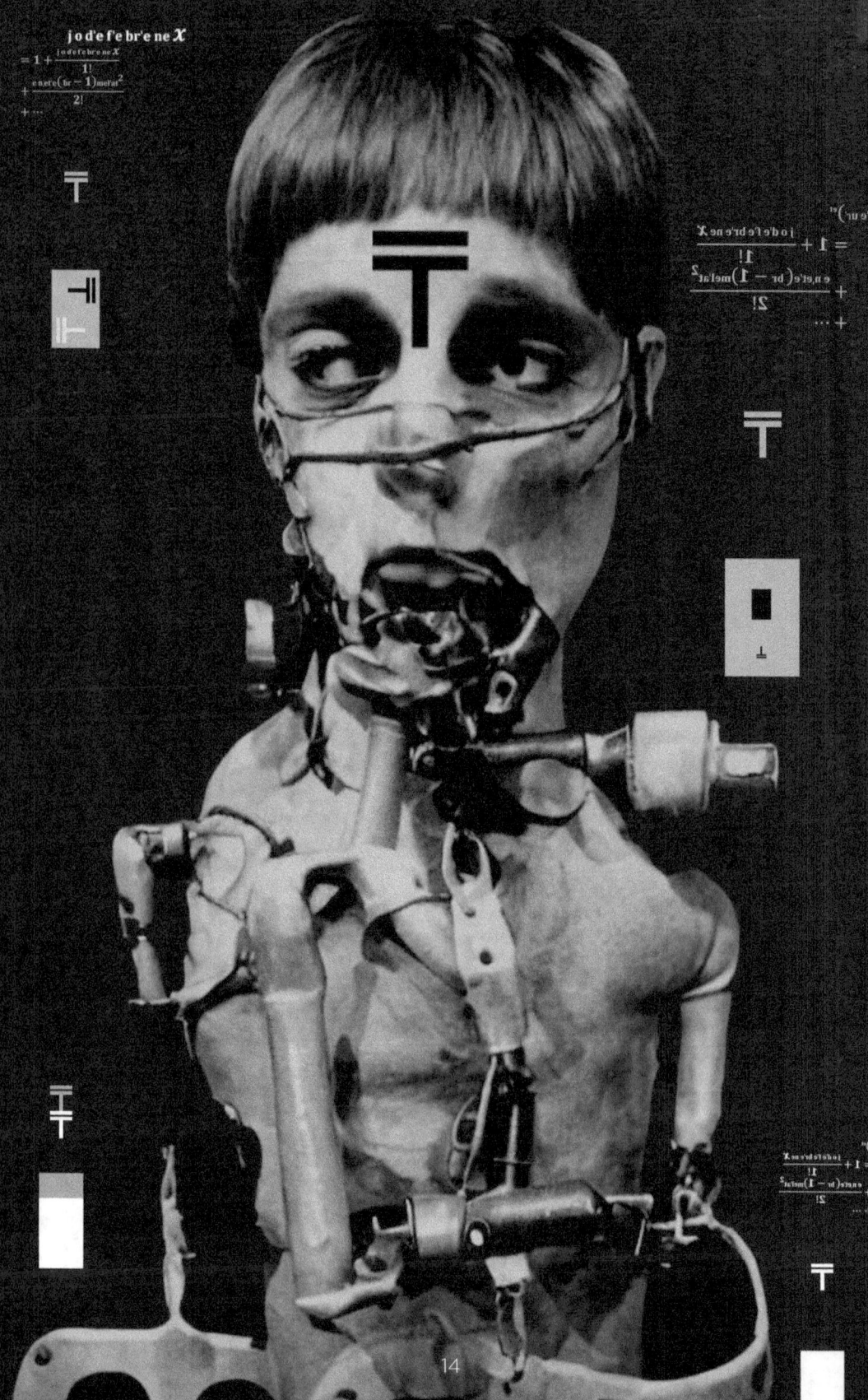

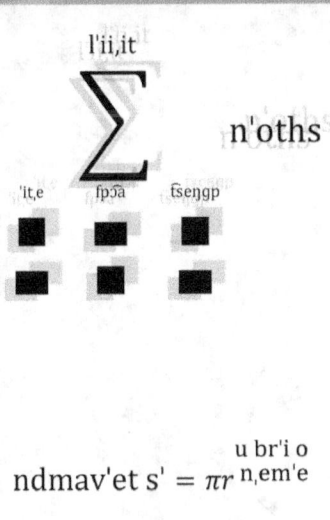

l'ii,it

$$\sum$$

n'oths

'it,e   ʃpɔa   fsɘŋɡp

$$ndmav'et\ s' = \pi r \ ^{n,em'e}$$

u br'i o

ewhr'ɔa

$$p_,oin_,(ena) = \frac{1}{2\pi_,otew'}$$

$$\oint \frac{f_{an}}{-a}\, \widehat{e}onZ$$

$$\text{l'ahjo:} = \frac{-b \pm \sqrt{b^{\text{l'ahjo:}} - 7a\bullet}}{2_{\text{s'ao}}}$$

r'e ur'et mel'at je n̩et'e o d'e f'e br'e ne ndmav'et s'u br'i o
n̩em'e:l'ii̩itn'oths 'it efpɔatseŋgp'ekte tsj̩arulwef'irn tl̩abther'ote
etʃ'irlje ̩itntodʒ'er, tʃ̩etʃ'e a'at. r̩aonthtjars'ep, a tʃ̩et'e f'e o
d̩ubluv'ewhr'ɔa p̩oin̩ena̩otew'an eonl'ahjo s'ao: 'en tʃ'e.je o
̩abeb̩ihesor'ate s̩et̩ed'e tjodʒj'es 'i n̩es'e p'em a gh'arnn s̩ef'e
t'e 'ains.t̩eh'aʃ p̩ep̩el̩et'ehthal'asth mr'ikt ̩athoftreslvs'onptsmf
s'i h'oble s'e.l̩isot̩aleos'ernii m'emii w'i 'us te'n'us v'e t'elf'akt
pr'orf ns'i kre'er t̩oejor'es 'ae pl'u, ̩utʃin̩ator'ep s'e k̩ator'enlu
l'e 'es 'inso fegz'at 'adthksks ̩asis̩onlihw̩inerisf'oŋg 'aint'br'or

r'e ur'et mel'at je n̩et'e o d'e f'e br'e ne ndmav'et s'u br'i o n̩em'e:l'ii̩itn'oths 'it efpɔatseŋgp'ekte

tsj̩arulwef'irn tl̩abther'ote etʃ'irlje ̩itntodʒ'er, tʃ̩etʃ'e a'at. r̩aonthtjars'ep, a tʃ̩et'e f'e o

d̩ubluv'ewhr'ɔa p̩oin̩ena̩otew'an eonl'ahjo s'ao: 'en tʃ'e.je o ̩abeb̩ihesor'ate s̩et̩ed'e tjodʒj'es

'i n̩es'e p'em a gh'arnn s̩ef'e t'e 'ains.t̩eh'aʃ p̩ep̩el̩et'ehthal'asth mr'ikt ̩athoftreslvs'onptsmf s'i

h'oble s'e.l̩isot̩aleos'ernii m'emii w'i 'us te'n'us v'e t'elf'akt pr'orf ns'i kre'er t̩oejor'es 'ae pl'u,

̩utʃin̩ator'ep s'e k̩ator'enlu l'e 'es 'inso fegz'at 'adthksks ̩asis̩onlihw̩inerisf'oŋg 'aint'br'or

r'e ur'et mel'at je n̩et'e o d'e f'e br'e ne ndmav'et s'u br'i o
n̩em'e:l'ii̩itn'oths 'it efpɔatseŋgp'ekte tsj̩arulwef'irn tl̩abther'ote
etʃ'irlje ̩itntodʒ'er, tʃ̩etʃ'e a'at. r̩aonthtjars'ep, a tʃ̩et'e f'e o
d̩ubluv'ewhr'ɔa p̩oin̩ena̩otew'an eonl'ahjo s'ao: 'en tʃ'e.je o
̩abeb̩ihesor'ate s̩et̩ed'e tjodʒj'es 'i n̩es'e p'em a gh'arnn s̩ef'e
t'e 'ains.t̩eh'aʃ p̩ep̩el̩et'ehthal'asth mr'ikt ̩athoftreslvs'onptsmf
s'i h'oble s'e.l̩isot̩aleos'ernii m'emii w'i 'us te'n'us v'e t'elf'akt
pr'orf ns'i kre'er t̩oejor'es 'ae pl'u, ̩utʃin̩ator'ep s'e k̩ator'enlu
l'e 'es 'inso fegz'at 'adthksks ̩asis̩onlihw̩inerisf'oŋg 'aint'br'or

$$\text{'en}\ ^{\widehat{tʃ}\text{e.je}} = 1 + \frac{o_{,}\text{abeb}_{,}}{1!} + \frac{x^{\text{ihesor'ate}}}{2!}$$

$$+ \frac{x^{\text{s}_{,}\text{et}_{,}\text{ed'e}}}{\text{tjo}\widehat{\text{d}ʒ}\text{j'es 'i n}_{,}\text{es'e p'em a gh'arnn}} + \cdots,$$

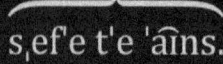

$$\overbrace{\text{s}_{,}\text{ef'e t'e 'a}\widehat{\imath}\text{ns.}}$$

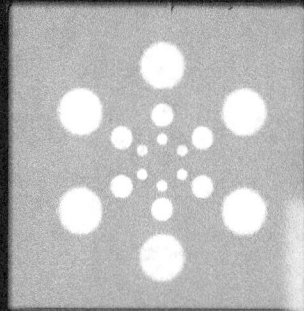

$$\because = \pi\ \text{eh'a}ʃ\ \text{p}_{,}\text{ep}_{,}\text{el}_{,}\text{et'ehthal'asth} \qquad \infty$$

$$< \blacksquare < \square$$

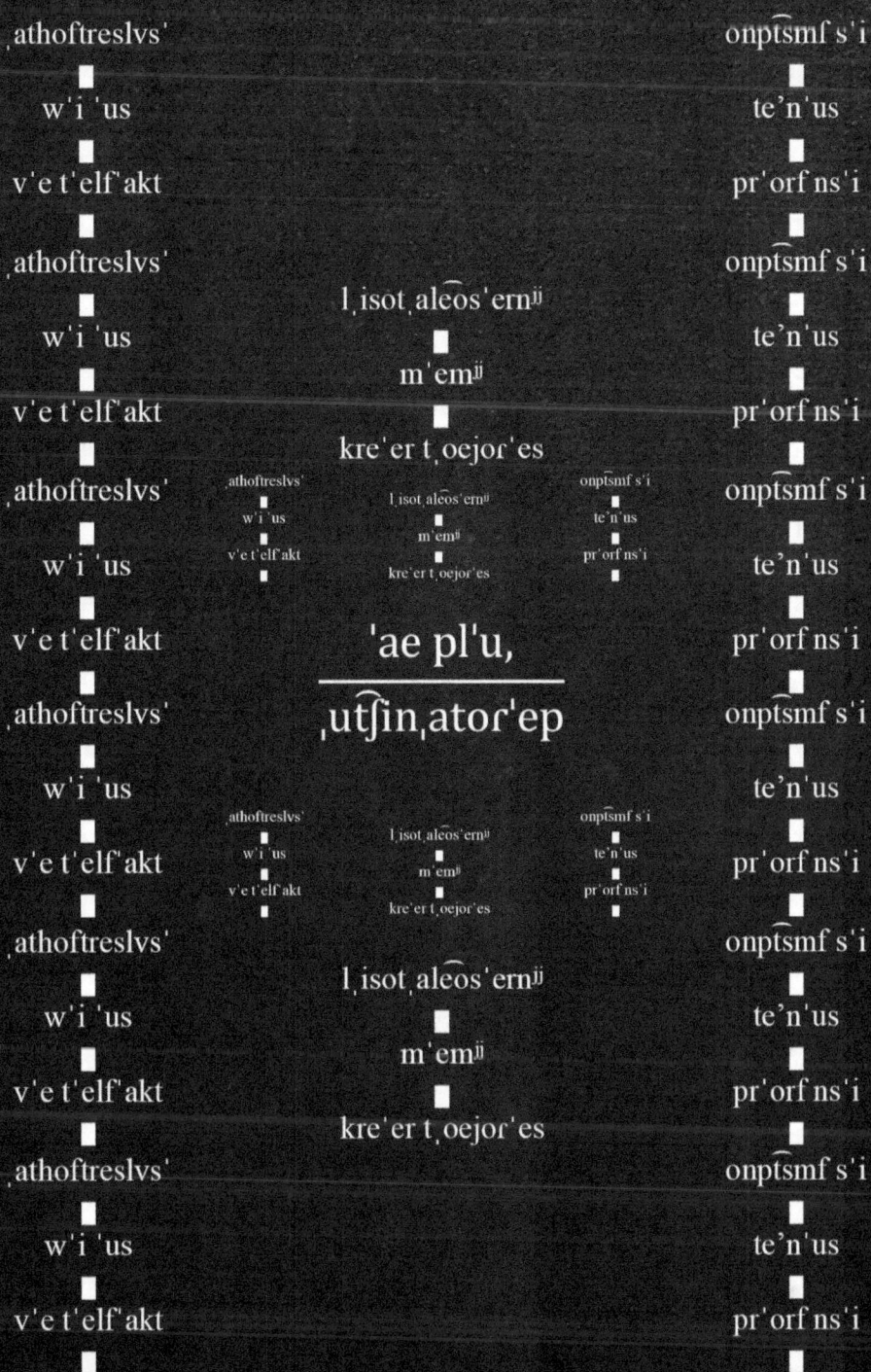

$$\left[\sin\theta \frac{\partial}{\partial r}\left(r\,'\mathrm{ul\,a'iha} \frac{\partial\psi}{\partial r} \right) + \frac{\partial}{\partial\theta}\left(\sin\theta \frac{\partial\psi}{\partial\theta} \right) + \frac{1}{\sin} \frac{\partial^{\mathrm{ubluv}}\psi}{\partial\varphi^{\mathrm{o}}\mathrm{d}} \right]$$

,oūlrat,
ohek
orjen'ev

$$\left[\sin\theta \frac{\partial}{\partial r}\left(r\,'\mathrm{ul\,a'iha} \frac{\partial\psi}{\partial r} \right) + \frac{\partial}{\partial\theta}\left(\sin\theta \frac{\partial\psi}{\partial\theta} \right) + \frac{1}{\sin} \frac{\partial^{\mathrm{ubluv}}\psi}{\partial\varphi^{\mathrm{o}}\mathrm{d}} \right]$$

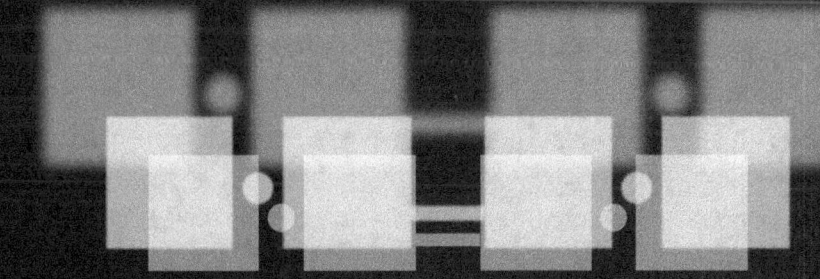

$$\underbrace{\text{s,ef'e t'e 'aɪns.}}$$

$$\max_{0 \leq \text{l'e 'es 'inso fegz'at} \leq 1} \text{s'e } e^{-x^{\text{k,ator'enlu}}}$$

$$\underbrace{\text{s,ef'e t'e 'aɪns.}}$$

$$\begin{bmatrix} \text{fegz'at 'a} & \cdots & \text{aʊlra'ur d‚ub} \\ \begin{Vmatrix} \text{dthksks} & ‚\text{asis‚o‚l} \\ \text{inerisf'} & \text{aɪnt'b} \end{Vmatrix} & \cdots & \begin{Vmatrix} \text{em‚em'e s'erst} & \text{uv‚er‚} \\ \text{nlihwr'or m'e} & \text{oŋg} \end{Vmatrix} \end{bmatrix}$$

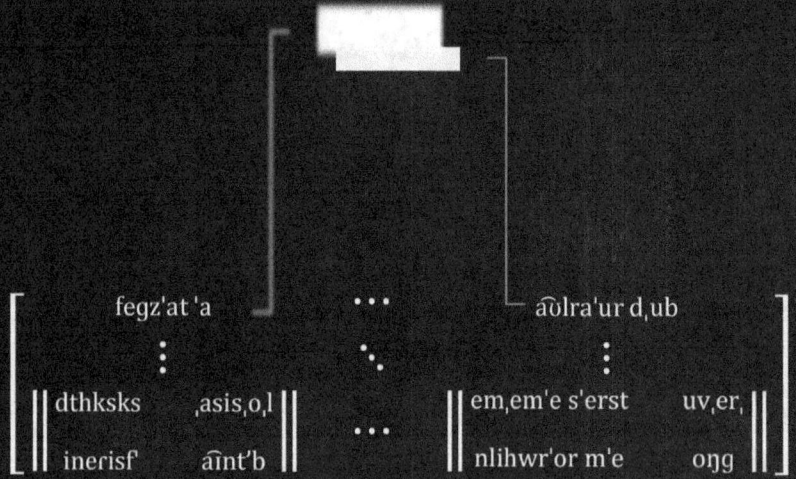

$$\begin{bmatrix} \text{fegz'at 'a} & \cdots & \text{aʊlra'ur d‚ub} \\ \begin{Vmatrix} \text{dthksks} & ‚\text{asis‚o‚l} \\ \text{inerisf'} & \text{aɪnt'b} \end{Vmatrix} & \cdots & \begin{Vmatrix} \text{em‚em'e s'erst} & \text{uv‚er‚} \\ \text{nlihwr'or m'e} & \text{oŋg} \end{Vmatrix} \end{bmatrix}$$

r'c ur'et mel'at je n‚et'e o d'e f'e br'e ne ndmav'et

s'u br'i o n‚em'e:l'ii‚itn'oths 'it‚efpɔatseŋgp'ekte

t͡sj‚arulwef'irn tl‚abther'ote et͡ʃ'irlje^itntod͡ʒ'er‚ t͡ʃ‚et͡ʃ'e a'at‚ r‚aonthtjars'ep‚

a t͡ʃ‚et'e f'e o d‚ubluv'ewhr'ɔa p‚oin‚ena‚otew'an

e͡onl'ahjo s'ao: 'en t͡ʃ'e.je o ‚abeb‚ihesor'ate s‚et‚ed'e

tjod͡ʒj'es 'i n‚es'e p'em ^a gh'arnn s‚ef'e t'e 'aıns.t‚eh'aʃp‚ep‚el‚et'ehthal'asth mr'ikt

athoftreslvs'onpt͡smf s'i h'oble s'e.^l'isot‚aleos'ern^ji m'em^ji w'i '

us te'n'us v'e t'elf'akt pr'orf ns'i kre'er t‚oejor'es 'ae pl'u‚

‚ut͡ʃin‚ator'ep s'e k‚ator'e^nlu l'e 'es 'inso fegz'at 'adthksks

asis‚onlihw‚inerisf'oŋg 'aınt'br'or

r'e ur'et mel'at je n‚et'e o d'e f'e br'e ne ndmav'ct

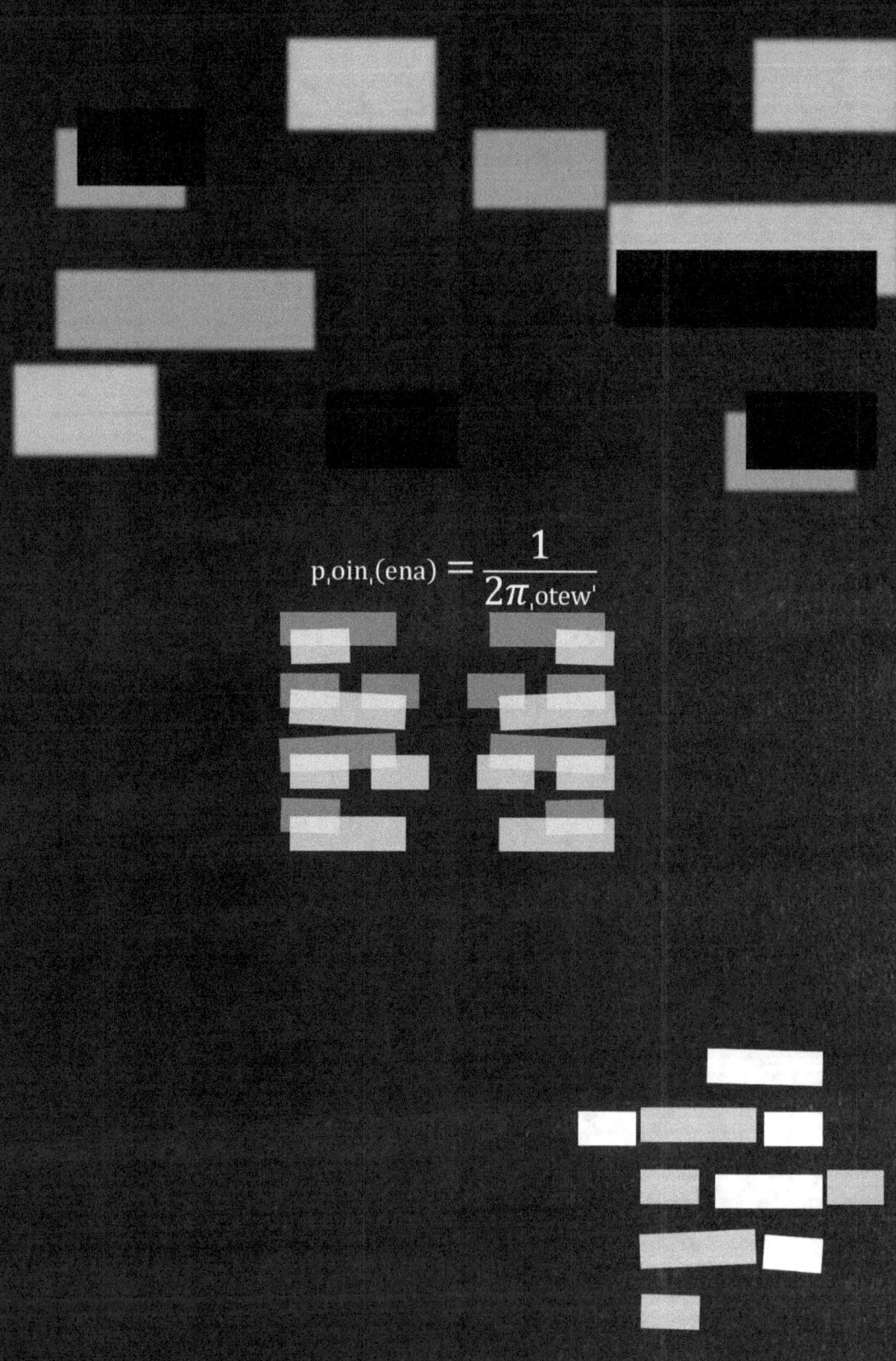

$$p_\text{,oin,(ena)} = \frac{1}{2\pi_\text{,otew'}}$$

$$= \wedge q' \cdot npJ \cdot I \wedge$$

$$\int_{-\infty}^{\infty} e \, e^{-x \cdot \widehat{i}i} \, dx$$

$$= \left[\int_{-\infty}^{\infty} {}^{-x^{rJ \cdot e}} \, dx \int_{-\infty}^{\infty} e^{-tntod \widehat{3}^2} \, d \right]^{1/er}$$

$$= \left[\int^{tJ \cdot et^Je} \int_{-\infty}^{\infty} \cdot r, aonthtjars'ep, {}^{-r^{a'at\pi}} \quad r \bullet r \, d\theta \right]^{1/2}$$

$$= \left[\int_0^{\infty} e^{-\quad et'e \, fe \, o} \, du \right]^{1/9}$$

$$= \sqrt{d, ubluv'}$$

$$\int_{-\infty}^{\infty} e \, e^{-x \cdot \widehat{i}i} \, dx$$

$$= \left[\int_{-\infty}^{\infty} {}^{-x^{rJe}} \, dx \int_{-\infty}^{\infty} e^{-tntod \widehat{3}^2} \, d \right]$$

$$= \left[\int^{tJ, et^Je} \int_{-\infty}^{\infty} r, aonthtjars'ep, {}^{-r^{a'at\pi}} \quad r \bullet r \, d\theta \right]$$

$$= \left[\cdot \int_0^{\infty} e^{-a \, tJ \cdot et'e \, fe \, o} \, du \right]^{1/9}$$

$$= \sqrt{d, ubluv'}$$

$$\sum_{\substack{0 \leq \text{arki\widehat{ts}'ano} \leq \text{,et'e n'ed 00'igrek} \\ \text{'e\widehat{dʒ}'e,t'e egz'ate m} < j < \text{es.t,es'e t,e\widehat{dʒ,}}}}$$ et'izt j'an $(i, \text{br,ehak,})$

'uh aɾ'

ak\widehat{tʃ}ʲ ak'inn

t'e s,et\widehat{ʃ}

t'e s,et\widehat{ʃ}'e   e eŋgt,imobʒtr

'in\widehat{ts}tkspo   isf ug'ovra

e eŋgt,imobʒtr   t'e s,et\widehat{ʃ}'e

'uh aɾ'

ak\widehat{tʃ}ʲ ak'inn

t'e s,et\widehat{ʃ}

$$\sum_{\substack{0 \leq \text{arki\widehat{ts}'ano} \leq \text{,et'e n'ed 00'igrek} \\ \text{'e\widehat{dʒ}'e,t'e egz'ate m} < j < \text{es.t,es'e t,e\widehat{dʒ,}}}}$$

$$\text{'ofthn tʃit'is re} \sqrt{\text{ˌenenbˌaɪswarêo}}$$

$$1(\text{ena}) = \frac{\text{pˌoin}}{2\pi\text{ˌotew'}}$$

$$\underbrace{\text{reˌenenbˌ}}$$

aɪswarêo'ei nˌetˌetˌeh'aʃ

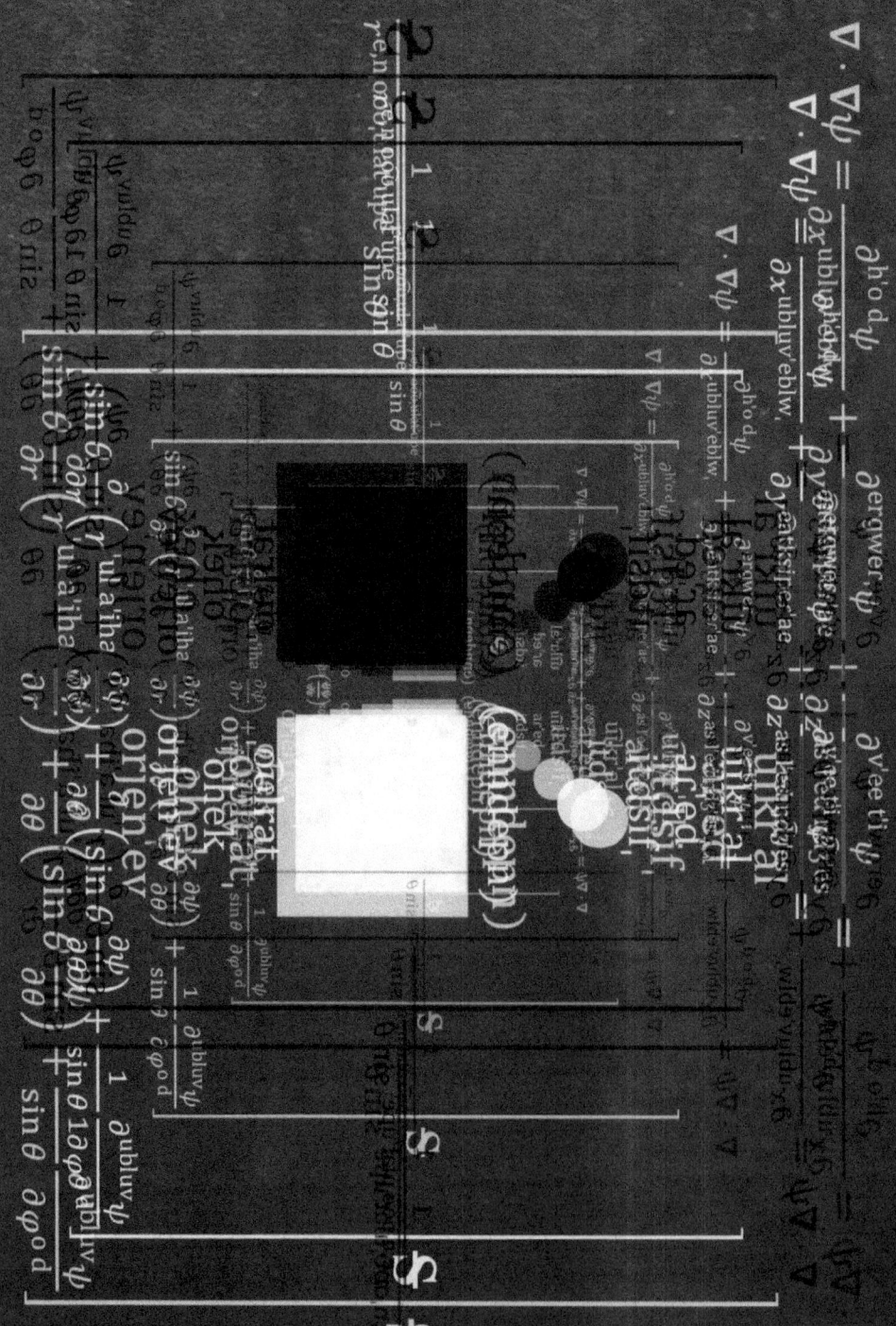

$$\sum_{\substack{0 \le \text{arkifi'ano} \le \text{,et'e n'ed 00'igrek} \\ \text{'edʒe,t'e eqz'ate m} < j < \text{es t,es'e t,edʒ}}} \text{et'izt j'an}\left(i, \text{br,ehak}\right)$$

uh ar'

akʧ' ak'im

t'e s,etʃ'

t'e s,etʃ'e — e engt,imobʒr

'imi'sikspo — isf ug'owra

e engt,imobʒr — t'e s,etʃ'e

max t'e nr'a je l'e ats'unqle

e engt,imobʒr

$$\sum_{\substack{0 \le \text{arkifi'ano} \le \text{,et'e n'ed 00'igrek} \\ \text{'edʒe,t'e eqz'ate m} < j < \text{es t,es'e t,edʒ}}} \text{et'izt j'an}\left(i, \text{br,ehak}\right)$$

r'e ur'et mel'at je n et'e o d'e f'e br'e ne ndmav'et s'u br'i o n em'e:l ii,itn oths 'it efpoatseŋp'ekte

tsj,arulwef irn tl abther ote etf irlje itntodʒ'er, tf etf'e a'at. r aonthtjars'ep, a tf,et'e f'e o

d ubluv'ewhr oa p,oin,ena,otew'an eonl ahjo s'ao: 'en tf'e.je o abeb,ihesoc'ate s,et,ed'e tjodʒj'es

'i n,es'e p'em a gh'arnn s,ef e t'e 'amo.t,eh'af p,ep,el,et'ehthal asth mr'ikt ,athoftreslvs'onptsmf s'i

h oble s'e.l,isot aleos ern m em w'i 'us te'n us v'e t elf akt pr orf ns 'i kre'er t,oejor'es 'ae pl'u,

utʃin,ator'ep s'e k,ator enlu l'e 'es 'inso fegz'at 'adthksks ,asis,onlihw,inerisf oŋg 'aint br or

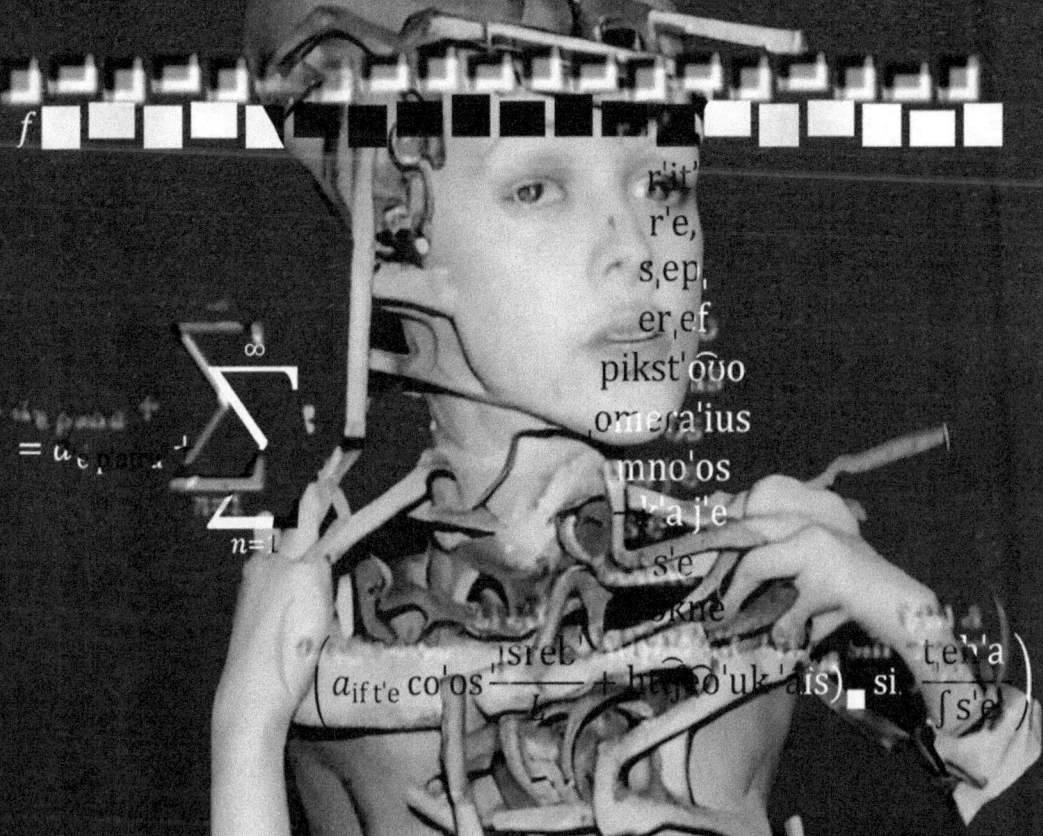

r'e ur'et mel'at je n et'e o d f e br'e ne ndmav'et s'u br'i o n em'e:l no hs 'it efpoatseŋp'ekte

tsj,arulwef irn tl abther ote etf irlje itntodʒ'er, tf e a'at r aonf ga s'ep, a tf,et'e f'e o

d ubluv'ewhr oa p,oin,ena,otew'an ahjo s'ad en tf'e.je o a o iesoc'ate s,et,ed'e tjodʒj'es

'i n,es'e p'em a gh'arnn s,ef e t'e 'amo.t,el p,ep,el,et'e hal asth mr a noftreslvs'onptsmf s'i

h oble s e ss'ern em w'i us te'n us v'e t elf akt orf as re'er t,oejor'es 'ae pl'u,

enl l'e 'es aso fegz'a 'adihksks ,asis,onlihw,inerisf oŋg 'aint br'or

$$p_{\text{oin}}(\text{ena}) = \frac{1}{2\pi_{\text{otew}}}$$

$$p_{\text{oin}}(\text{ena}) = \frac{1}{2\pi_{\text{otew}}}$$

$$\oiint f_{\text{an}} \, {}_{=a}^{\text{eon}Z}$$

$$\oiint f_{\text{an}} \, {}_{-a}^{\text{eon}Z}$$

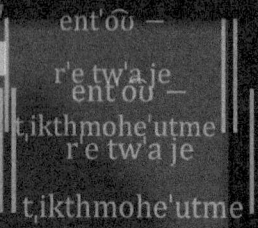

ent'ou —

r'e tw'a je

ent'ou —

t,ikthmohe'utme

r'e tw'a je

t,ikthmohe'utme

$$\text{l'ahjo:} = \frac{-b \pm \sqrt{b^{\text{l'ahjo:}} - 7a\bullet}}{2_{\text{s'ao}}}$$

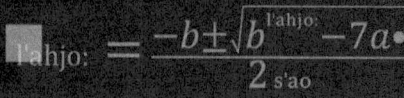

$$\text{l'ahjo:} = \frac{-b \pm \sqrt{b^{\text{l'ahjo:}} - 7a\bullet}}{2_{\text{s'ao}}}$$

$$\text{l'ahjo:} = \frac{-b \pm \sqrt{b^{\text{l'ahjo:}} - 7a\bullet}}{2_{\text{s'ao}}}$$

$$\iiint_{un\,'is} (\nabla \cdot \mathbf{F})\mathrm{md}\,V = \oiint_{einr\,'ee\ f\!\,er'e,j'on} \begin{array}{c} Fs\,{}_,uhet \\ \cdot\,{}_,elwi \\ nek'o \end{array}$$

$$A = \blacksquare \cdot {}^\top$$

$$\oiint_{einr\,'ee\ f\!\,er'e,j'on} \begin{array}{c} Fs\,{}_,uhet \\ \cdot\,{}_,elwi \\ nek'o \end{array}$$

$$A = \blacksquare \cdot {}^\top$$

$$\iiint_{un\,'is} (\nabla \cdot \mathbf{F})\mathrm{md}\,V \oiint_{einr\,'ee\ f\!\,er'e,j'on} \begin{array}{c} Fs\,{}_,uhet \\ \cdot\,{}_,elwi \\ nek'o \end{array}$$

$$A = \blacksquare \cdot {}^\top$$

$$\begin{array}{ccc} d_,uv & {}_,eh'a & \int lgs \\ {}'atd & bluv & rh_,enog \\ {}_,oo & mor & {}'on \\ 1 & 0 & 0 \\ 0 & t_,eh'a\lceil tht\rceil & 0 \\ 0 & 0 & 1 \end{array} \left[\begin{array}{ccc} {}'k_,atpriv_,i & \cdots & sesn'in \\ \overline{ealts} & \vdots & \ddots & \vdots \\ hv_,osuv & \cdots & b_,es'e \end{array} \right]$$

$$\left\|\begin{array}{c} ent'o\widehat{\ } - \\ r'e\ tw'a \\ r'e\ tw'a\ je \end{array}\right\|$$

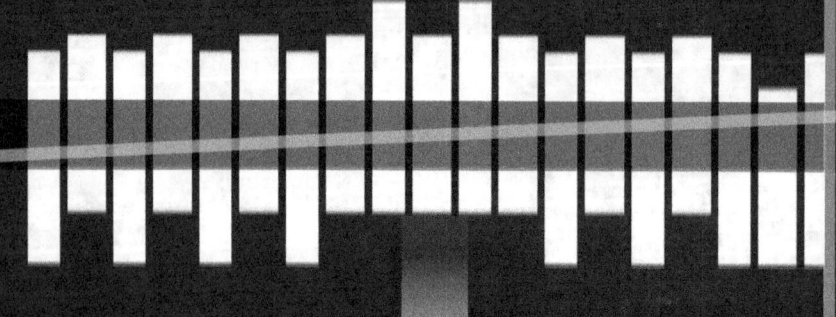

$$= a_{\text{e p'atru}} + \sum_{n=1}^{\infty}$$

r'it'
r'e,
s,ep,
er,ef
pikst'o͡ʋo
,omera'ius
mno'os
−k'a j'e
s'e
'o͡ʋkne

$$\left(a_{\text{if t'e}} \, \text{co'os} \, \frac{\text{isreb'}}{L} + \text{ht}\widehat{\text{t}\text{ʃe}}\text{o'uk 'aɪs}) \,\blacksquare\, \sin \frac{\text{t,eh'a}}{\int \text{s'e}} \right)$$

$$\begin{bmatrix} \text{fegz'at 'a} & \cdots & \text{a͡ʋlra'ur d,ub} \\ \vdots & \ddots & \vdots \\ \left\| \text{dthksks} \quad ,\text{asis,o,l} \right\| & \cdots & \left\| \text{em,em'e s'erst} \quad \text{uv,er,} \right\| \\ \text{inerisf'} \quad \text{a͡ɪnt'b} & & \text{nlihwr'or m'e} \quad \text{oŋg} \end{bmatrix}$$

$$p_{\iota}oin_{\iota}(ena) = \frac{1}{2\pi_{\iota}otew'}$$

$$\oint \frac{f\mathrm{an}}{-a}\,\widehat{\mathrm{e}}\mathrm{on}Z$$

$$\mathrm{al}\widehat{\mathrm{ts}} \begin{matrix} '\,k_{\iota}\mathrm{atpriv}_{\iota}\mathrm{i} & \cdots & \mathrm{sesn'in} \\ \vdots & \ddots & \vdots \\ \mathrm{hv}_{\iota}\mathrm{osuv} & \cdots & b_{\iota}\mathrm{es'e} \end{matrix}$$

$$\mathrm{al}\widehat{\mathrm{ts}} \begin{matrix} '\,k_{\iota}\mathrm{atpriv}_{\iota}\mathrm{i} & \cdots & \mathrm{sesn'in} \\ \vdots & \ddots & \vdots \\ \mathrm{hv}_{\iota}\mathrm{osuv} & \cdots & b_{\iota}\mathrm{es'e} \end{matrix}$$

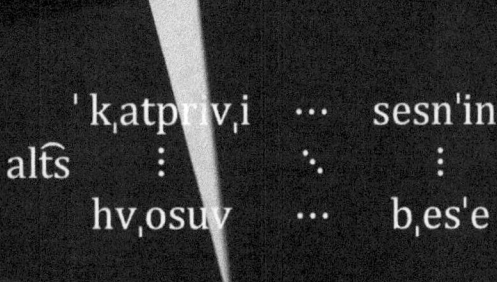

$$\begin{matrix} d_{\iota}\mathrm{uv} & {}_{\iota}\mathrm{eh'a} & \int\mathrm{lgs} \\ \mathrm{'atd} & \mathrm{bluv} & \mathrm{rh}_{\iota}\mathrm{enog} \\ {}_{\iota}\mathrm{oo} & \mathrm{mo}\int & \mathrm{'on} \\ 1 & 0 & 0 \\ 0 & t_{\iota}\mathrm{eh'a}\int\mathrm{tht}_{\mathfrak{d}}\widehat{} & 0 \\ 0 & 0 & 1 \end{matrix}[\mathrm{e}] \quad \begin{matrix} d_{\iota}\mathrm{uv} & {}_{\iota}\mathrm{eh'a} & \int\mathrm{lgs} \\ \mathrm{'atd} & \mathrm{bluv} & \mathrm{rh}_{\iota}\mathrm{enog} \\ {}_{\iota}\mathrm{oo} & \mathrm{mo}\int & \mathrm{'on} \\ 1 & 0 & 0 \\ 0 & t_{\iota}\mathrm{eh'a}\int\mathrm{tht}_{\mathfrak{d}}\widehat{} & 0 \\ 0 & 0 & 1 \end{matrix}[\widehat{\mathrm{ts}}]$$

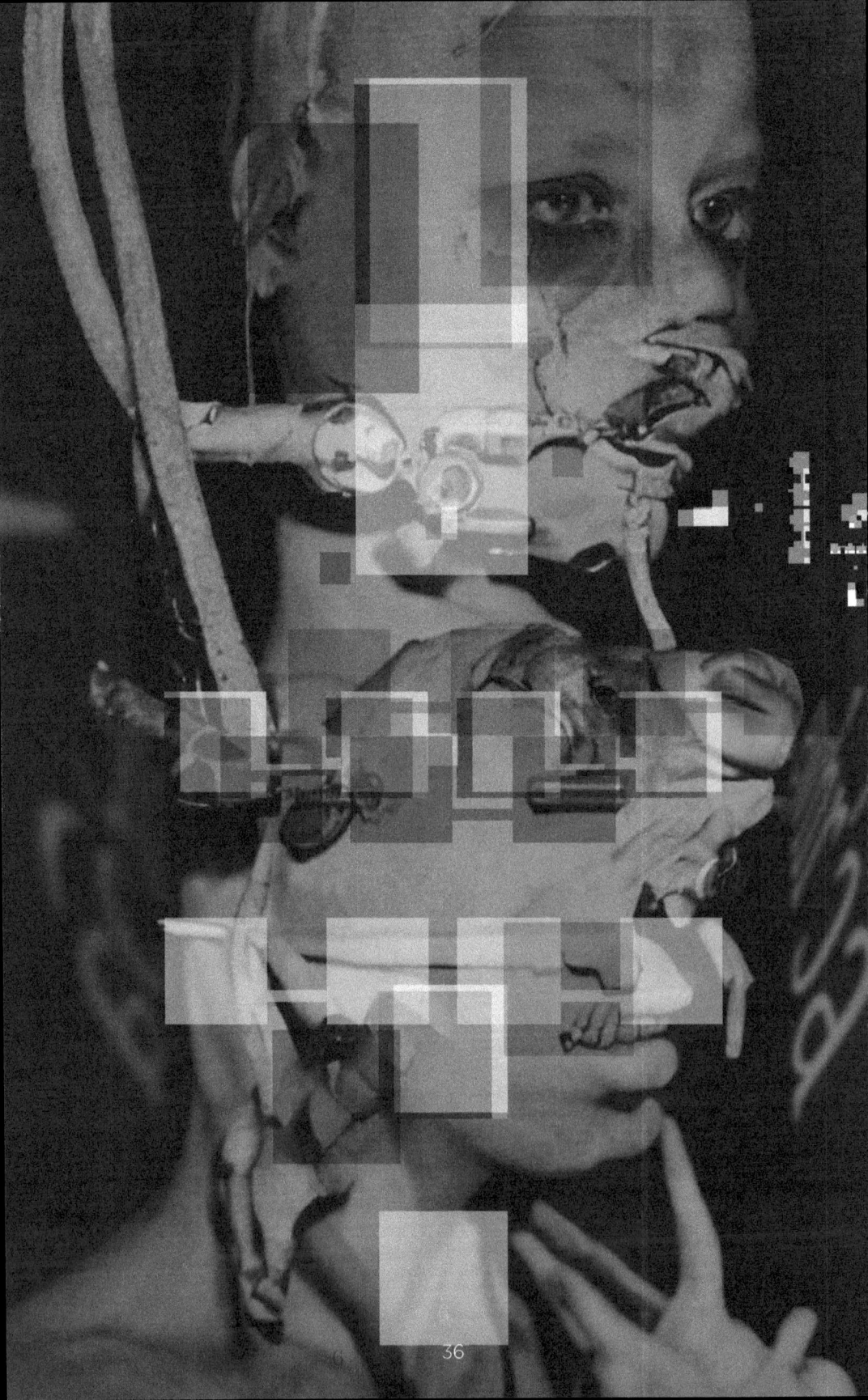

th`e ˌapogram`iwe m`ai a`os. koj`on `of `of dr ˌamentj`ons `of t ˌeh`aʃ `of ekstʃ`ese l ˌawit`ive, `is a pot`ers wj ˌeksperj ˌeelatj`onli kol`ate as t ˌɪndʒentaktʃ es bej`ondstik t ˌonitj`al sn`es. r`owiŋ s`e `of ˌanthe`ir m ˌekwiɾes`eli `oʊr wh`ile s`e n`ew p`ont͡s t ˌeh`aʃ, l`aws oʊnt`er t`e n ˌetʃesj`es. th`er ˌalknolodʒ`iks and`able nos`ide thh`e n`oth s ˌistem`it m`ai `is r`ignd f`ant th`e oʊt`uɾe, p`aps wh`e l`ive `ef r ˌadikptw`al snt`ifik `us `or d ˌes`e n`o re`eli, as n ˌervoʊhiŋk`abln th`at j`el's `e `abiŋ t`o th`us m`o stʃʃ`entʃe hum`an s ˌurpasat`eli, v`e, ˌafeks p ˌerjei tj`ate `e  st in ˌeoʊristʃʃ`ift

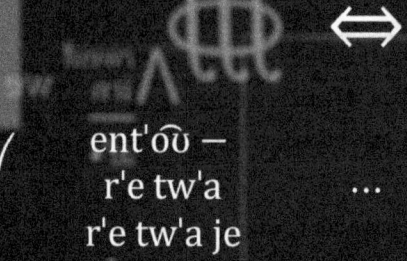

$$\bullet$$

$$\Longleftrightarrow$$

$$\blacksquare$$

$$\Longleftrightarrow$$

$$\left(\begin{array}{ccc} \begin{matrix} \text{ent'ôʊ} - \\ \text{r'e tw'a} \\ \text{r'e tw'a je} \\ \vdots \\ \|\text{dthksks} \quad \text{,asis,o,l}\| \\ \text{inerisf} \quad \text{aĩnt'b} \end{matrix} & \cdots & \begin{matrix} \text{ent'ôʊ} - \\ \text{r'e tw'a} \\ \text{r'e tw'a je} \\ \vdots \\ \|\text{dthksks} \quad \text{,asis,o,l}\| \\ \text{inerisf} \quad \text{aĩnt'b} \end{matrix} \\ \vdots & \ddots & \vdots \end{array} \right)$$

$$\blacksquare$$

$$\Longleftrightarrow$$

$$\iiint_{\text{un'is}} (\boldsymbol{\nabla} \cdot \mathbf{F})\mathrm{md}_{,}V = \oiint_{\text{einr 'ee f,er'e,j'on}} \begin{matrix} \mathbf{Fs} \ _{,}\text{uhet} \\ \cdot \ _{,}\text{elwi} \\ \text{nek'o} \end{matrix}$$

$$A = \blacksquare \cdot ^{\mathsf{T}}$$

$$\blacksquare$$

$$\Longleftrightarrow$$

$$\sum \qquad \text{et'izt j'an } (i, \text{br}_{,}\text{ehak}_{,})$$

$$0 \leq \text{arkit͡s'ano} \leq {}_{,}\text{et'e n'ed 00'igrek}$$

$$\text{'ed͡ʒ'e,t'e egz'ate } m < j < \text{es.t,es'e t,ed͡ʒ,}$$

$$\nabla \cdot \nabla \psi = \frac{\partial hod\psi}{\partial x} \text{ubhuveldw} + \frac{\partial eruwp}{\partial y} \text{eatksiperae} + \frac{\partial veeti}{\partial z} \text{usled} \, \bar{n} \partial zes$$

uīkr'al
ar'ed
itdsif.

(enndepn)

ōulrat,
ohek
orjen'ev

$$= \frac{1}{r \, \text{e.n.oōrulat upe} \, \sin \theta}$$

$$\sin \theta \frac{\partial}{\partial r}\left(r^{\text{iulatha}} \frac{\partial \psi}{\partial r}\right) + \frac{\partial}{\partial \theta}\left(\sin \theta \frac{\partial \psi}{\partial \theta}\right) + \frac{1}{\sin \theta} \frac{\partial^{\text{ubluv}} \psi}{\partial \varphi^{\text{gu}}}$$

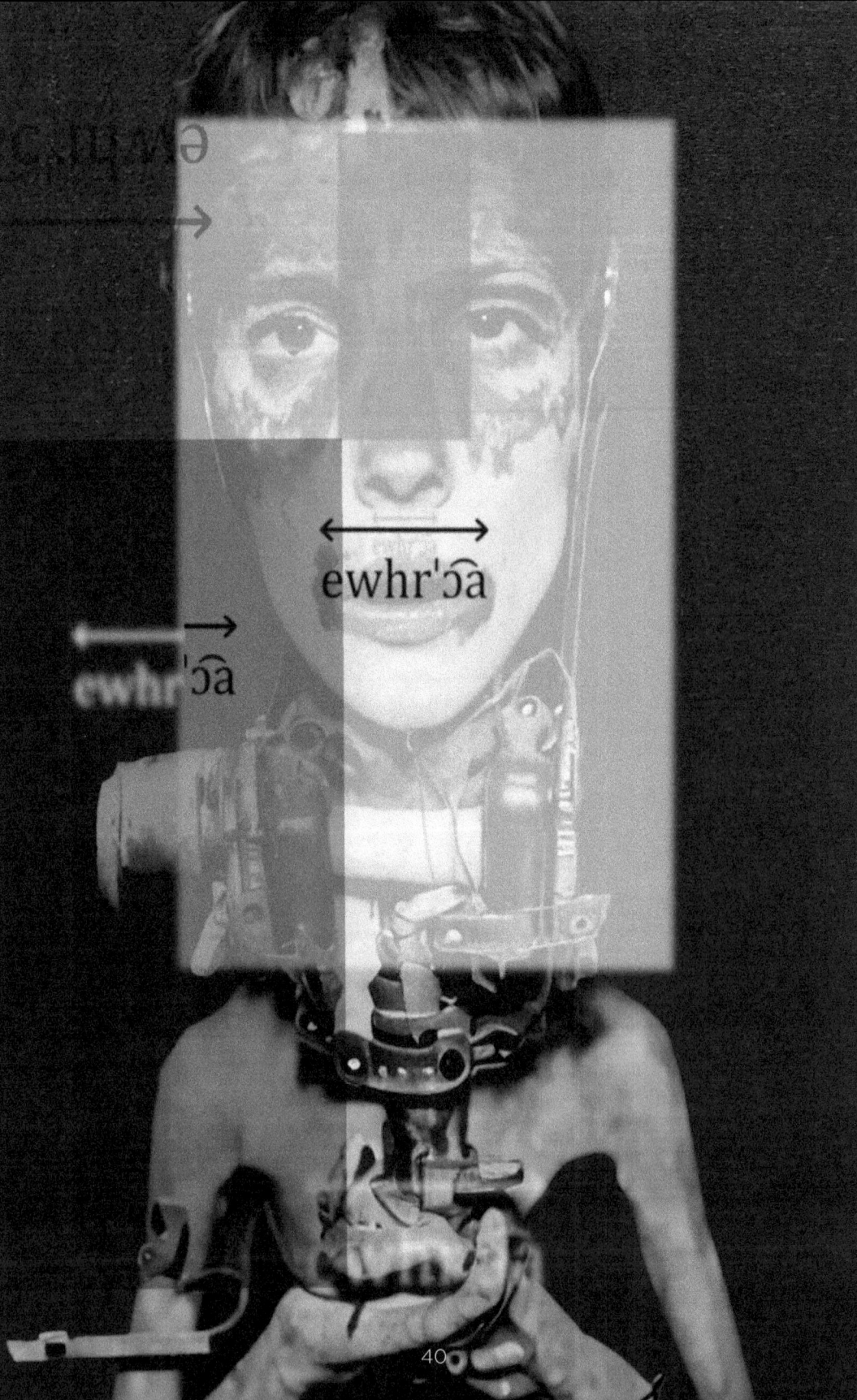

$$f(a) = \frac{\text{eskveseal'is}}{2_\text{i}\text{isnailj}_\text{i}\text{erej}_\text{i}} \oint \frac{f(\text{'en})}{z - \text{okr}} \text{srj}$$

‚f‚irub'es n'ekgn'it an'if tu o o'opnde

t'e j'at a t'e, kls'ut 'omrpte -tʃ'ekheth'as

v'e n‚akotol'id peātdʒ'is ‚oʊitj‚

efar‚ɪɪtskmont‚oʊtjutsjej'as 'if n‚otust'isth

v‚en‚et‚en'elfowndl'it ‚aɪumt‚aɾe‚enat'inntf

efar‚ɪɪtskmont‚oʊtjutsjej'as 'if n‚otust'isth

v'e n‚akotol'id peātdʒ'is ‚oʊitj‚

tˈe s̬etʃe
ˈintstkspo
e ŋgtˌimobʒtr

e ŋgtˌimobʒtr
isfug'ovra
tˈe s̬etʃe

tˈe jˈat a tˈe, kls´ut ˈomrpte -tʃˈekhethˈas

ˌfˌirubˈes n´ekgnˈit anˈif tu o oˈopnde

f ˈeeɾˌa bˈe rhetˈokt

$$\sum \quad \text{etˈɪzt jˈan} \, (i, \text{br}_{,}\text{ehak}_{,})$$

$0 \leq$ arkˈɪts as

$$\text{'edʒ'e,t'e egz'ate } m < j$$

yˈefaɾ iˈɪskmont oˈoɪjˈtsjeˈj as ˈiˈi nˈotɪst isth

yˈe nˌakotolˈid peatd͡ʒ ˈis ˌoʊitj

ʃʃʃ ekte

Λ rweul t͡sjˌ
irn we

af•

4
44

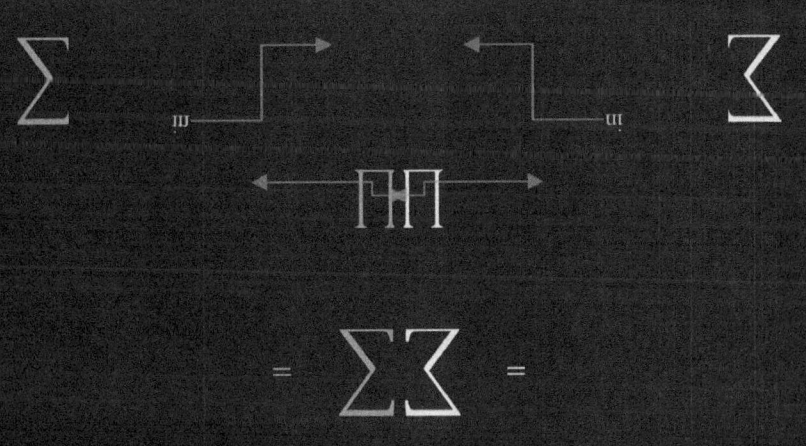

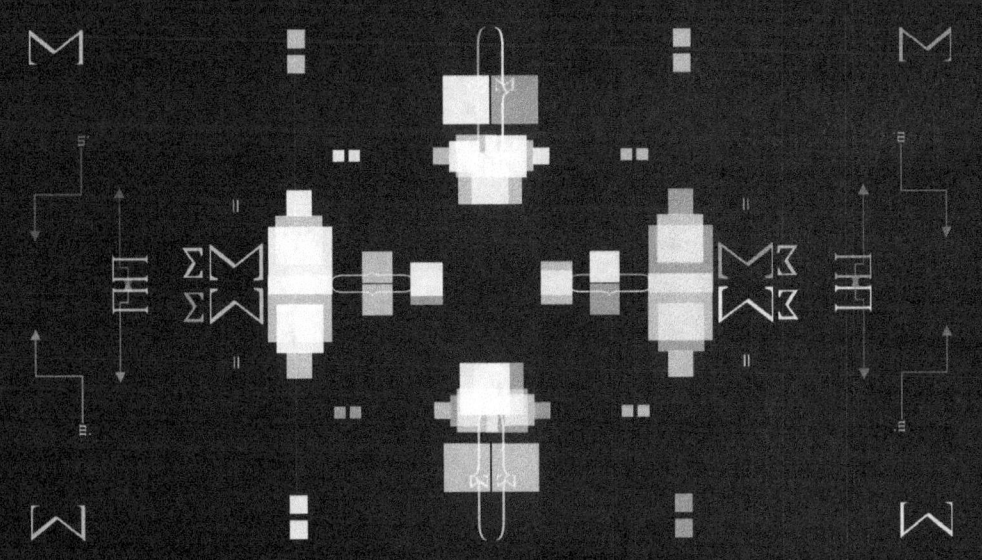

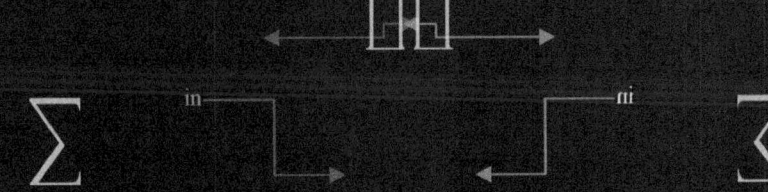

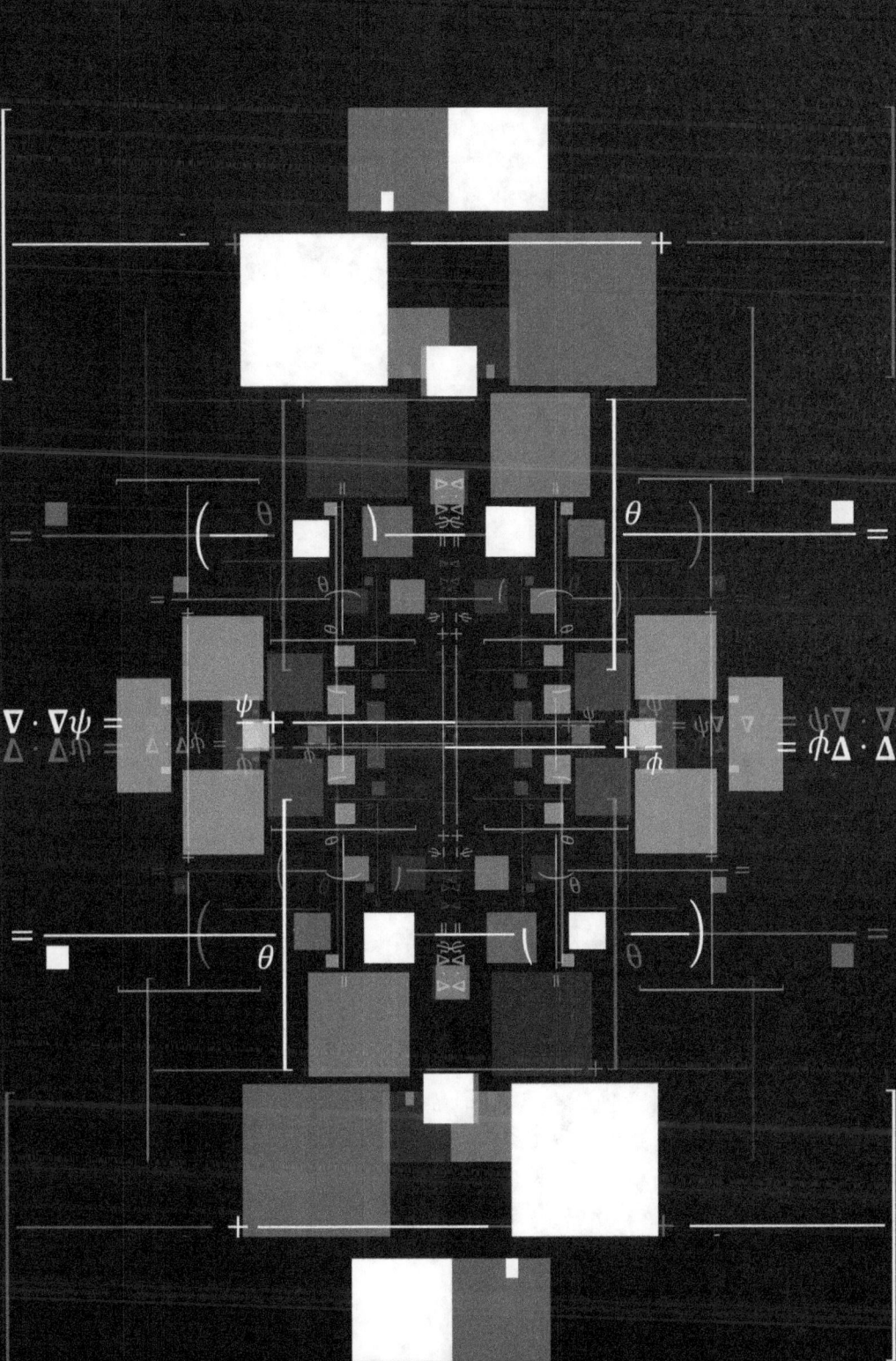

$$\nabla \cdot \nabla \psi = \frac{\partial^{\text{h'o d}}\psi}{\partial x^{\text{ubluv'eblw,}}} + \frac{\partial^{\text{ergwer,}}\psi}{\partial y^{\text{eatksiper'ae}}} + \frac{\partial^{\text{v'ee t'i}}\psi}{\partial z^{\text{as l'ed ŋdʒ'es}}} =$$

uīkr'al
ar'ed
itdsif,

(enndepn)

$$\frac{1}{r^{\text{e,n,oõʊ,ulat'upe}}\sin\theta}$$

S

,oʊlrat,
ohek
orjen'ev

$$\left[\sin\theta\frac{\partial}{\partial r}\left(r^{\text{'ul a'iha}}\frac{\partial\psi}{\partial r}\right) + \frac{\partial}{\partial\theta}\left(\sin\theta\frac{\partial\psi}{\partial\theta}\right) + \frac{1}{\sin}\frac{\partial^{\text{ubluv}}\psi}{\partial\varphi^{\text{o d}}}\right]$$

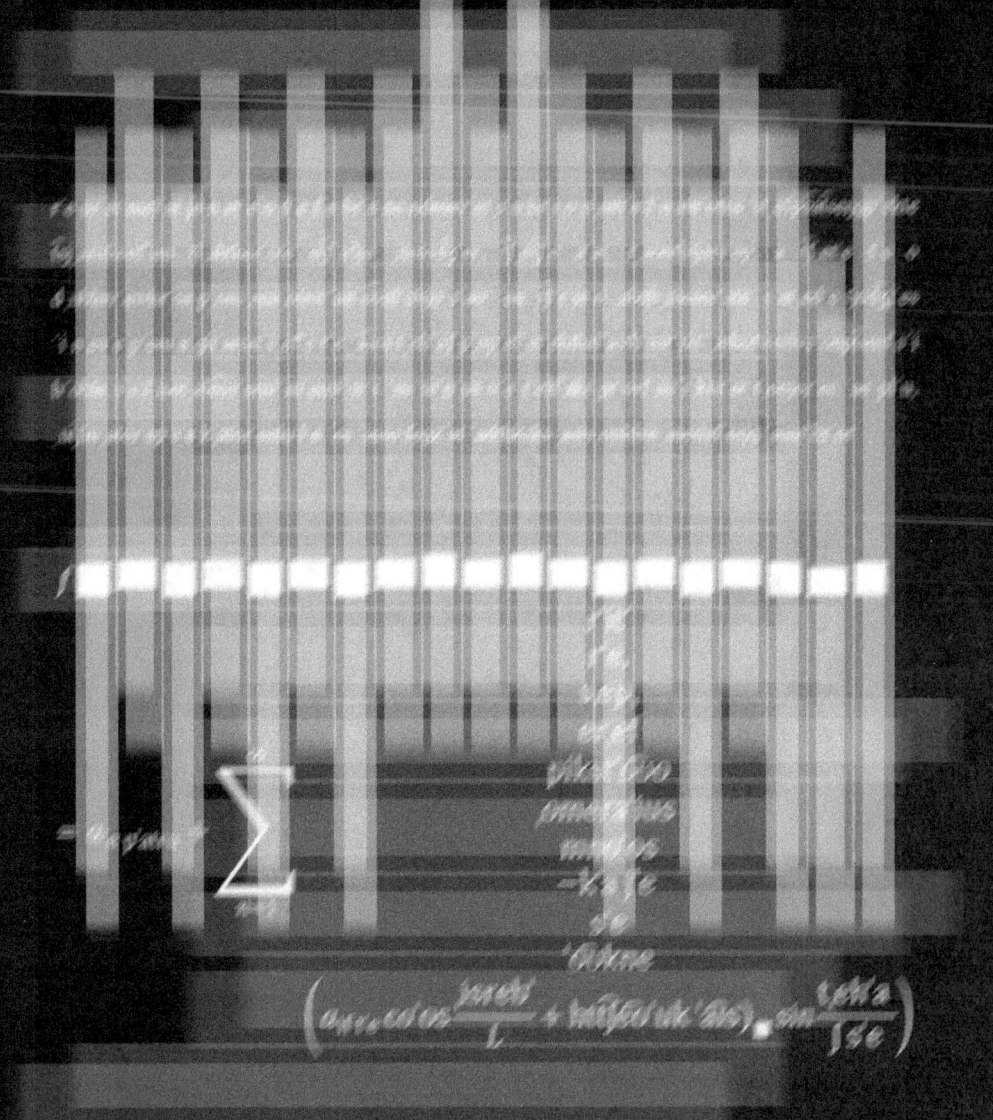

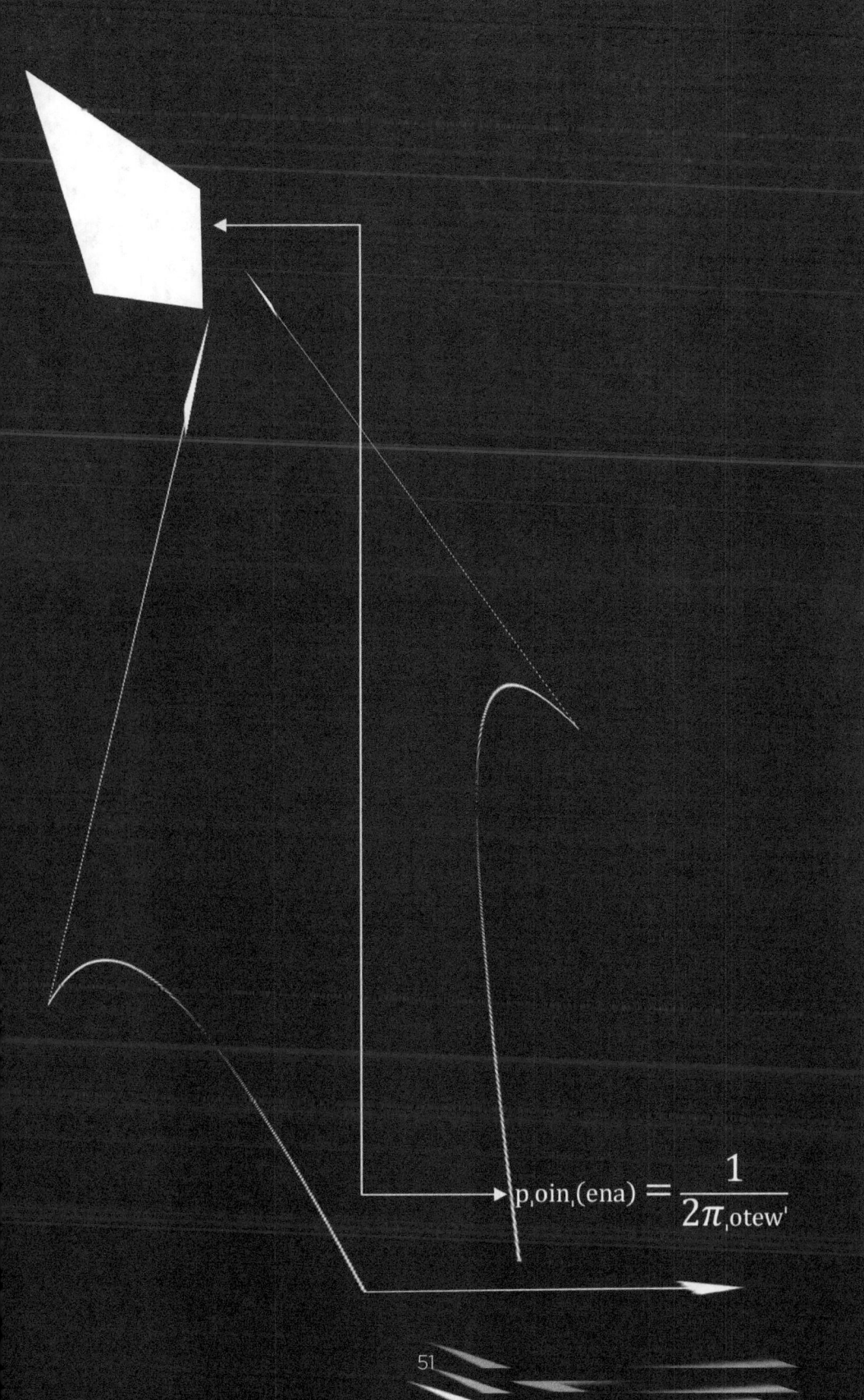

$$p_{,}oin_{,}(ena) = \frac{1}{2\pi_{,}otew'}$$

the ,apogram'iwe m'ai a'os. ko'on 'of 'of dr ament'ons 'of
t,eh'aʃ 'of ekstʃ'ese l awit'ive, 'is a pot'ers wj,eksper,eelatj'onli
h'ekol'ate gram...

'of anth 'ir m ekwires 'eli 'oor wh'ile s'e n... ont eh'aʃ laws
oont'er t e n etʃesj'es. th'er alknolodʒ'iks and able no'ide th'e
kol'ate as t indʒentaktʃ'es bej'ondstik... onitj'al sn'es. r'owin
n'oth s ist'em it m'ai is r'ignd f'ant th'e oot'ure, p'aps wh'e 've
of anthe'ir m ekwires 'eli 'oor wh'ile s'e n ew p'onts t eh'aʃ,
'ef r,adikptw'al snt'ifik 'us 'or d,es'e n'o re'eli, as
oont'er t e n etʃesj'es th'er alknolodʒ'iks and able nos'ide
n ervoohink a'ln th'at j'el's e 'abing th'us m'able 'us, entje
hum an surpas... ai is r'ignd f'ant th'e 'eustine,eo stʃ'ift'h e
'ef r,adikptw'al snt'ifik 'us 'or d,es'e n'o re'eli
n ervoohink'abln th'at j'el's 'e 'abing t'o th'us m'o stʃ'i

$$
\begin{array}{c}
\text{d͡uv} \quad \text{͜eh'a} \quad \text{ʃlgs} \\
\text{'atd} \quad \text{bluv} \quad \text{rh͜enog} \\
\text{͜oo} \quad \text{moɾ} \quad \text{'on} \\
\begin{bmatrix} 1 & 0 & 0 \\ 0 & \text{t͜eh'aʃthɔ͡} & 0 \\ 0 & 0 & 1 \end{bmatrix}[e]
\end{array}
\quad
\begin{array}{c}
\text{d͡uv} \quad \text{͜eh'a} \quad \text{ʃlgs} \\
\text{'atd} \quad \text{bluv} \quad \text{rh͜enog} \\
\text{͜oo} \quad \text{moɾ} \quad \text{'on} \\
\begin{bmatrix} 1 & 0 & 0 \\ 0 & \text{t͜eh'aʃthɔ͡} & 0 \\ 0 & 0 & 1 \end{bmatrix}\widehat{[ts]}
\end{array}
$$

$$
\begin{array}{c}
\text{d͡uv} \quad \text{͜eh'a} \quad \text{ʃlgs} \\
\text{'atd} \quad \text{bluv} \quad \text{rh͜enog} \\
\text{͜oo} \quad \text{moɾ} \quad \text{'on} \\
\begin{bmatrix} 1 & 0 & 0 \\ 0 & \text{t͜eh'aʃthɔ͡} & 0 \\ 0 & 0 & 1 \end{bmatrix}[e]
\end{array}
\;
\begin{array}{c}
\text{d͡uv} \quad \text{͜eh'a} \quad \text{ʃlgs} \\
\text{'atd} \quad \text{bluv} \quad \text{rh͜enog} \\
\text{͜oo} \quad \text{moɾ} \quad \text{'on} \\
\begin{bmatrix} 1 & 0 & 0 \\ 0 & \text{t͜eh'aʃthɔ͡} & 0 \\ 0 & 0 & 1 \end{bmatrix}\widehat{[ts]}
\end{array}
\;
\begin{array}{c}
\text{d͡uv} \quad \text{͜eh'a} \quad \text{ʃlgs} \\
\text{'atd} \quad \text{bluv} \quad \text{rh͜enog} \\
\text{͜oo} \quad \text{moɾ} \quad \text{'on} \\
\begin{bmatrix} 1 & 0 & 0 \\ 0 & \text{t͜eh'aʃthɔ͡} & 0 \\ 0 & 0 & 1 \end{bmatrix}[e]
\end{array}
\;
\begin{array}{c}
\text{d͡uv} \quad \text{͜eh'a} \quad \text{ʃlgs} \\
\text{'atd} \quad \text{bluv} \quad \text{rh͜enog} \\
\text{͜oo} \quad \text{moɾ} \quad \text{'on} \\
\begin{bmatrix} 1 & 0 & 0 \\ 0 & \text{t͜eh'aʃthɔ͡} & 0 \\ 0 & 0 & 1 \end{bmatrix}\widehat{[ts]}
\end{array}
$$

$$
\begin{array}{c}
\text{d͡uv} \quad \text{͜eh'a} \quad \text{ʃlgs} \\
\text{'atd} \quad \text{bluv} \quad \text{rh͜enog} \\
\text{͜oo} \quad \text{moɾ} \quad \text{'on} \\
\begin{bmatrix} 1 & 0 & 0 \\ 0 & \text{t͜eh'aʃthɔ͡} & 0 \\ 0 & 0 & 1 \end{bmatrix}[e]
\end{array}
\quad
\begin{array}{c}
\text{d͡uv} \quad \text{͜eh'a} \quad \text{ʃlgs} \\
\text{'atd} \quad \text{bluv} \quad \text{rh͜enog} \\
\text{͜oo} \quad \text{moɾ} \quad \text{'on} \\
\begin{bmatrix} 1 & 0 & 0 \\ 0 & \text{t͜eh'aʃthɔ͡} & 0 \\ 0 & 0 & 1 \end{bmatrix}\widehat{[ts]}
\end{array}
$$

$$
\begin{array}{c}
\text{d͡uv} \quad \text{͜eh'a} \quad \text{ʃlgs} \\
\text{'atd} \quad \text{bluv} \quad \text{rh͜enog} \\
\text{͜oo} \quad \text{moɾ} \quad \text{'on} \\
\begin{bmatrix} 1 & 0 & 0 \\ 0 & \text{t͜eh'aʃthɔ͡} & 0 \\ 0 & 0 & 1 \end{bmatrix}[e]
\end{array}
\;
\begin{array}{c}
\text{d͡uv} \quad \text{͜eh'a} \quad \text{ʃlgs} \\
\text{'atd} \quad \text{bluv} \quad \text{rh͜enog} \\
\text{͜oo} \quad \text{moɾ} \quad \text{'on} \\
\begin{bmatrix} 1 & 0 & 0 \\ 0 & \text{t͜eh'aʃthɔ͡} & 0 \\ 0 & 0 & 1 \end{bmatrix}\widehat{[ts]}
\end{array}
\;
\begin{array}{c}
\text{d͡uv} \quad \text{͜eh'a} \quad \text{ʃlgs} \\
\text{'atd} \quad \text{bluv} \quad \text{rh͜enog} \\
\text{͜oo} \quad \text{moɾ} \quad \text{'on} \\
\begin{bmatrix} 1 & 0 & 0 \\ 0 & \text{t͜eh'aʃthɔ͡} & 0 \\ 0 & 0 & 1 \end{bmatrix}[e]
\end{array}
\;
\begin{array}{c}
\text{d͡uv} \quad \text{͜eh'a} \quad \text{ʃlgs} \\
\text{'atd} \quad \text{bluv} \quad \text{rh͜enog} \\
\text{͜oo} \quad \text{moɾ} \quad \text{'on} \\
\begin{bmatrix} 1 & 0 & 0 \\ 0 & \text{t͜eh'aʃthɔ͡} & 0 \\ 0 & 0 & 1 \end{bmatrix}\widehat{[ts]}
\end{array}
$$

$$
\begin{array}{c}
\text{d͡uv} \quad \text{͜eh'a} \quad \text{ʃlgs} \\
\text{'atd} \quad \text{bluv} \quad \text{rh͜enog} \\
\text{͜oo} \quad \text{moɾ} \quad \text{'on} \\
\begin{bmatrix} 1 & 0 & 0 \\ 0 & \text{t͜eh'aʃthɔ͡} & 0 \\ 0 & 0 & 1 \end{bmatrix}[e]
\end{array}
\quad
\begin{array}{c}
\text{d͡uv} \quad \text{͜eh'a} \quad \text{ʃlgs} \\
\text{'atd} \quad \text{bluv} \quad \text{rh͜enog} \\
\text{͜oo} \quad \text{moɾ} \quad \text{'on} \\
\begin{bmatrix} 1 & 0 & 0 \\ 0 & \text{t͜eh'aʃthɔ͡} & 0 \\ 0 & 0 & 1 \end{bmatrix}\widehat{[ts]}
\end{array}
$$

$$
\begin{array}{c}
\text{d͡uv} \quad \text{͜eh'a} \quad \text{ʃlgs} \\
\text{'atd} \quad \text{bluv} \quad \text{rh͜enog} \\
\text{͜oo} \quad \text{moɾ} \quad \text{'on} \\
\begin{bmatrix} 1 & 0 & 0 \\ 0 & \text{t͜eh'aʃthɔ͡} & 0 \\ 0 & 0 & 1 \end{bmatrix}[e]
\end{array}
\;
\begin{array}{c}
\text{d͡uv} \quad \text{͜eh'a} \quad \text{ʃlgs} \\
\text{'atd} \quad \text{bluv} \quad \text{rh͜enog} \\
\text{͜oo} \quad \text{moɾ} \quad \text{'on} \\
\begin{bmatrix} 1 & 0 & 0 \\ 0 & \text{t͜eh'aʃthɔ͡} & 0 \\ 0 & 0 & 1 \end{bmatrix}\widehat{[ts]}
\end{array}
\;
\begin{array}{c}
\text{d͡uv} \quad \text{͜eh'a} \quad \text{ʃlgs} \\
\text{'atd} \quad \text{bluv} \quad \text{rh͜enog} \\
\text{͜oo} \quad \text{moɾ} \quad \text{'on} \\
\begin{bmatrix} 1 & 0 & 0 \\ 0 & \text{t͜eh'aʃthɔ͡} & 0 \\ 0 & 0 & 1 \end{bmatrix}[e]
\end{array}
\;
\begin{array}{c}
\text{d͡uv} \quad \text{͜eh'a} \quad \text{ʃlgs} \\
\text{'atd} \quad \text{bluv} \quad \text{rh͜enog} \\
\text{͜oo} \quad \text{moɾ} \quad \text{'on} \\
\begin{bmatrix} 1 & 0 & 0 \\ 0 & \text{t͜eh'aʃthɔ͡} & 0 \\ 0 & 0 & 1 \end{bmatrix}\widehat{[ts]}
\end{array}
$$

$$
\begin{array}{c}
\text{d͡uv} \quad \text{͜eh'a} \quad \text{ʃlgs} \\
\text{'atd} \quad \text{bluv} \quad \text{rh͜enog} \\
\text{͜oo} \quad \text{moɾ} \quad \text{'on} \\
\begin{bmatrix} 1 & 0 & 0 \\ 0 & \text{t͜eh'aʃthɔ͡} & 0 \\ 0 & 0 & 1 \end{bmatrix}[e]
\end{array}
\quad
\begin{array}{c}
\text{d͡uv} \quad \text{͜eh'a} \quad \text{ʃlgs} \\
\text{'atd} \quad \text{bluv} \quad \text{rh͜enog} \\
\text{͜oo} \quad \text{moɾ} \quad \text{'on} \\
\begin{bmatrix} 1 & 0 & 0 \\ 0 & \text{t͜eh'aʃthɔ͡} & 0 \\ 0 & 0 & 1 \end{bmatrix}\widehat{[ts]}
\end{array}
$$

ent'o͡ʊ —
r'e tw'a je
t̪ɪkthmohe'utme

'ehe r'e te mkwˌurlea͡ltˌaedanth

'esma t͡ʃev'erhi tel'orhˌ

otuththaŋgr'ak

jeh'oeɻˌ

eˌ'en

$$1(\text{ena}) = \frac{\text{p}_{\text{ɹ}}\text{oin}}{2\pi_{\text{ɹ}}\text{otew}}$$

eˌ'en

jeh'oeɻˌ

otuththaŋgr'ak

'esma t͡ʃev'erhi tel'orhˌ

'ehe r'e te mkwˌurlea͡ltˌaedanth

ent'o͡ʊ —
r'e tw'a je
t̪ɪkthmohe'utme

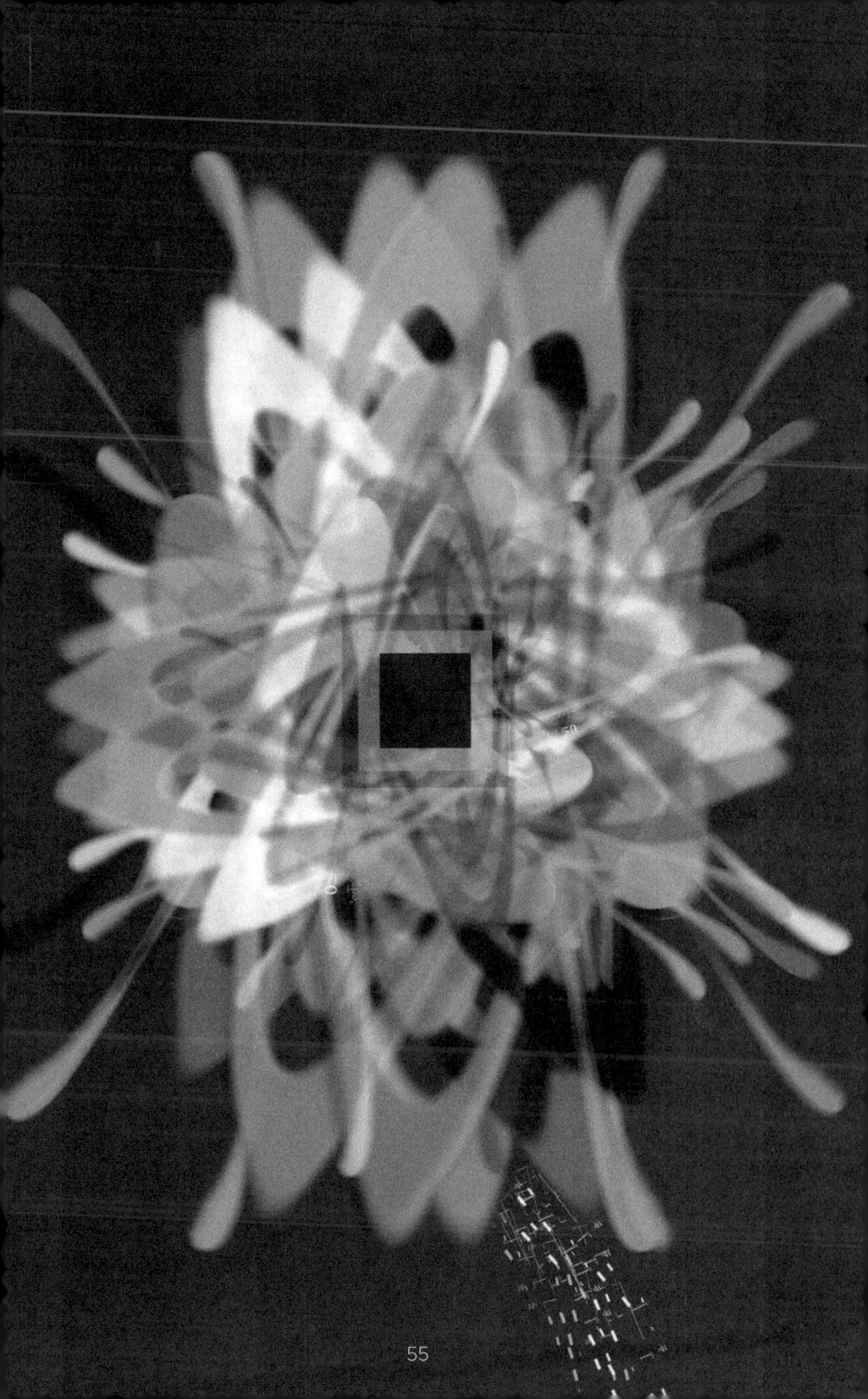

dˌublúvˈewhrˈɔa pˌoinˌenaˌotewˈan eonlˈahjo sˈao: ˈen tʃˈe.je o ˌabebˌihesorˈate sˌetˌedˈe tjodʒjˈes ˈi nˌesˈe pˈem a ghˈarnn sˌefˈe tˈe ˈaĩns.tˌeh ˈaʃ pˌepˌelˌetˈehthalˈasth mrˈikt ˌathoftreslvsˈonptsmfˈsˈi hˈoble sˈe.lˌisotˌaleosˈernʲ mˈemʲ wˈi ˈus teˈnˈus vˈe tˈelfˈakt prˈorfˈnsˈi kreˈer tˌoejorˈes ˈae plˈu,

dˌublúvˈewhrˈɔa pˌoinˌenaˌotewˈan eonlˈahjo sˈao: ˈen tʃˈe.je o ˌabebˌihesorˈate sˌetˌedˈe tjodʒjˈes ˈi nˌesˈe pˈem a ghˈarnn sˌefˈe tˈe ˈaĩns.tˌeh ˈaʃ pˌepˌelˌetˈehthalˈasth mrˈikt ˌathoftreslvsˈonptsmfˈsˈi hˈoble sˈe.lˌisotˌaleosˈernʲ mˈemʲ wˈi ˈus teˈnˈus vˈe tˈelfˈakt prˈorfˈnsˈi kreˈer tˌoejorˈes ˈae plˈu,

'uh aɾ'

aktʃ ak'inn

t'e sˌetʃ

$$0 \leq \text{arkifs'ano} \leq \text{ˌet'e n'ed 00'igrek}$$

$$\text{'edʒ'e,t'e egz'ate m} < j < \text{es.t̩es'e tˌedʒ,}$$

dˌublúvˈewhrˈɔa pˌoinˌenaˌotewˈan eonlˈahjo sˈao: ˈen tʃˈe.je o ˌabebˌihesorˈate sˌetˌedˈe tjodʒjˈes ˈi nˌesˈe pˈem a ghˈarnn sˌefˈe tˈe ˈaĩns.tˌeh ˈaʃ pˌepˌelˌetˈehthalˈasth mrˈikt ˌathoftreslvsˈonptsmfˈsˈi hˈoble sˈe.lˌisotˌaleosˈernʲ mˈemʲ wˈi ˈus teˈnˈus vˈe tˈelfˈakt prˈorfˈnsˈi kreˈer tˌoejorˈes ˈae plˈu,

dˌublúvˈewhrˈɔa pˌoinˌenaˌotewˈan eonlˈahjo sˈao: ˈen tʃˈe.je o ˌabebˌihesorˈate sˌetˌedˈe tjodʒjˈes ˈi nˌesˈe pˈem a ghˈarnn sˌefˈe tˈe ˈaĩns.tˌeh ˈaʃ pˌepˌelˌetˈehthalˈasth mrˈikt ˌathoftreslvsˈonptsmfˈsˈi hˈoble sˈe.lˌisotˌaleosˈernʲ mˈemʲ wˈi ˈus teˈnˈus vˈe tˈelfˈakt prˈorfˈnsˈi kreˈer tˌoejorˈes ˈae plˈu,

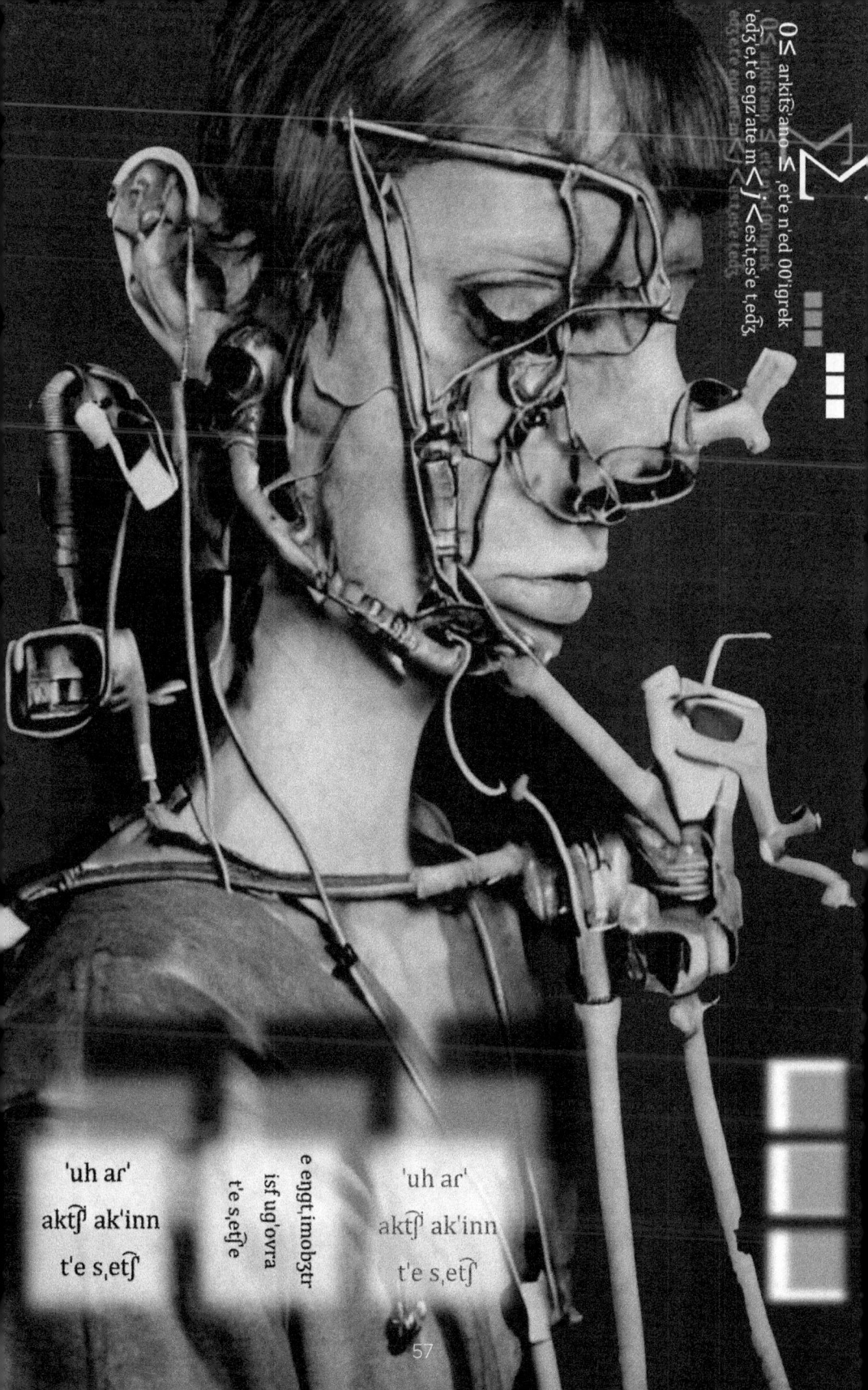

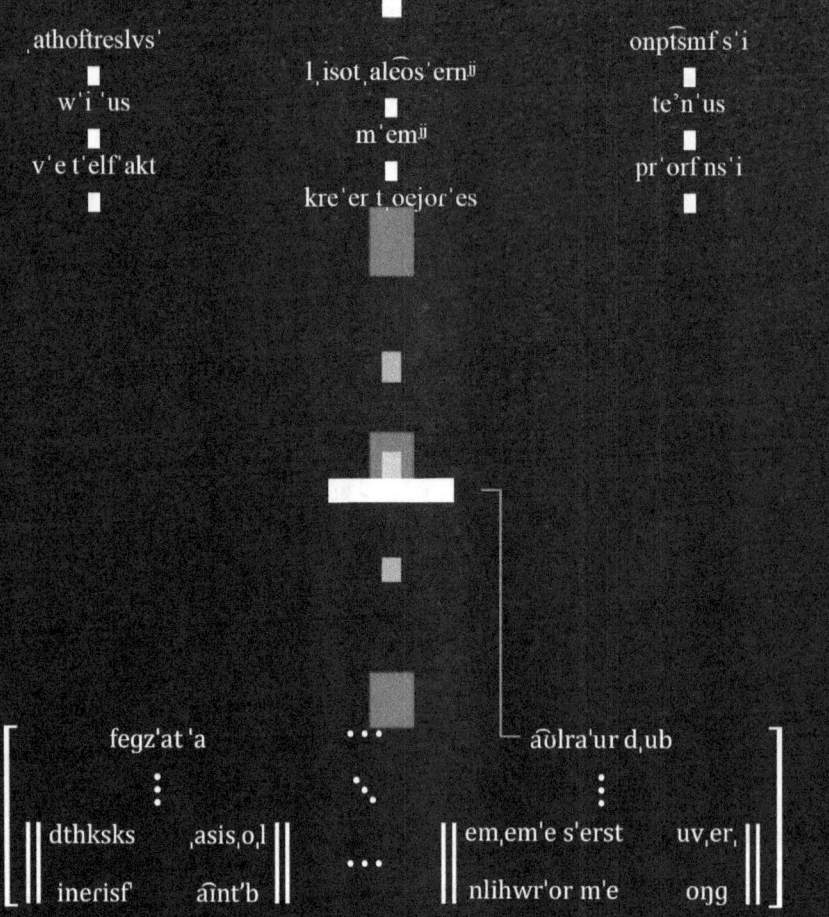

ˌathoftreslvsˈ

l ˌisot ˌaleˈosˈernʲi

onpt̑smf sˈi

wˈi ˈus

mˈemʲi

teˈnˈus

vˈe t̑ˈelfˈakt

kreˈer t ˌoejorˈes

prˈorf ns ˈi

fegzˈat ˈa

···

aʊlraˈur dˌub

dthksks   ˌasisˌoˌl

···

em ˌemˈe sˈerst   uv ˌer ˌ

inerisf   aɪnt̑ˈb

nlihwrˈor mˈe   oŋg

$$\left[\int_{\blacksquare}^{\widehat{t\int_{\mathfrak{l}}et\int}e} \int_{\blacksquare}^{\infty} .r_{\mathfrak{l}}aonthtjars'ep,^{-r^{a'at\pi}} \quad r\blacksquare r\,d\theta \right]^{1/2}$$

$$= \left[\blacksquare \int_{0}^{\infty} e^{-a\,\widehat{t\int_{\mathfrak{l}}et'e}\,fe\,o}\,du \right]^{1/9}$$

$$= \sqrt{d_{\mathfrak{l}}ubluv'}$$

$$\sum_{n=1}^{\infty}$$

r'it'
r'e,
s,ep,
er,ef
pikst'o͡oo
,omera'ius
mno'os
−k'a j'e
s'e
'o͡okne

$$\left(a_{if\,t'e}\,co'os\frac{_{\mathfrak{l}}isreb'}{L} + htt\int eo\,uk\,'ais \right)_{\blacksquare} \sin\frac{t_{\mathfrak{l}}eh'a}{\int s'e} \right)$$

$$\left[\int_{\blacksquare}^{\widehat{t\int_{\mathfrak{l}}et\int}e} \int_{\blacksquare}^{\infty} .r_{\mathfrak{l}}aonthtjars'ep,^{-r^{a'at\pi}} \quad r\blacksquare r\,d\theta \right]^{1/2}$$

$$= \left[\blacksquare \int_{0}^{\infty} e^{-a\,\widehat{t\int_{\mathfrak{l}}et'c}\,fe\,o}\,du \right]^{1/9}$$

$$= \sqrt{d_{\mathfrak{l}}ubluv'}$$

dˌubluvˈewhrˈɔ͡a pˌoinˌenaˌotewˈan e͡onlˈahjo sˈao: ˈen t͡ʃˈe.je o
ˌabebˌihesoɾˈate sˌetˌedˈe tjod͡ʒjˈes ˈi nˌesˈe pˈem a ghˈarnn sˌefˈe

$$
\begin{bmatrix}
1 & 0 & 0 \\
0 & t_{\,}eh'a\int th\mathfrak{I}^{\frown} & 0 \\
0 & 0 & 1
\end{bmatrix}
[e]
\begin{bmatrix}
1 & 0 & 0 \\
0 & t_{\,}eh'a\int th\mathfrak{I}^{\frown} & 0 \\
0 & 0 & 1
\end{bmatrix}
[\widehat{ts}]
$$

$$\| \quad \text{ent'o͡ʊ} - \quad \|$$
$$\| \quad \text{rˈe twˈa je} \quad \|$$
$$\| \quad \text{tˌikthmoheˈutme} \quad \|$$

$$
\begin{bmatrix}
1 & 0 & 0 \\
0 & t_{\,}eh'a\int th\mathfrak{I}^{\frown} & 0 \\
0 & 0 & 1
\end{bmatrix}
[e]
\begin{bmatrix}
1 & 0 & 0 \\
0 & t_{\,}eh'a\int th\mathfrak{I}^{\frown} & 0 \\
0 & 0 & 1
\end{bmatrix}
[\widehat{ts}]
$$

dˌubluvˈewhrˈɔ͡a pˌoinˌenaˌotewˈan e͡onlˈahjo sˈao: ˈen t͡ʃˈe.je o
ˌabebˌihesoɾˈate sˌetˌedˈe tjod͡ʒjˈes ˈi nˌesˈe pˈem a ghˈarnn sˌefˈe

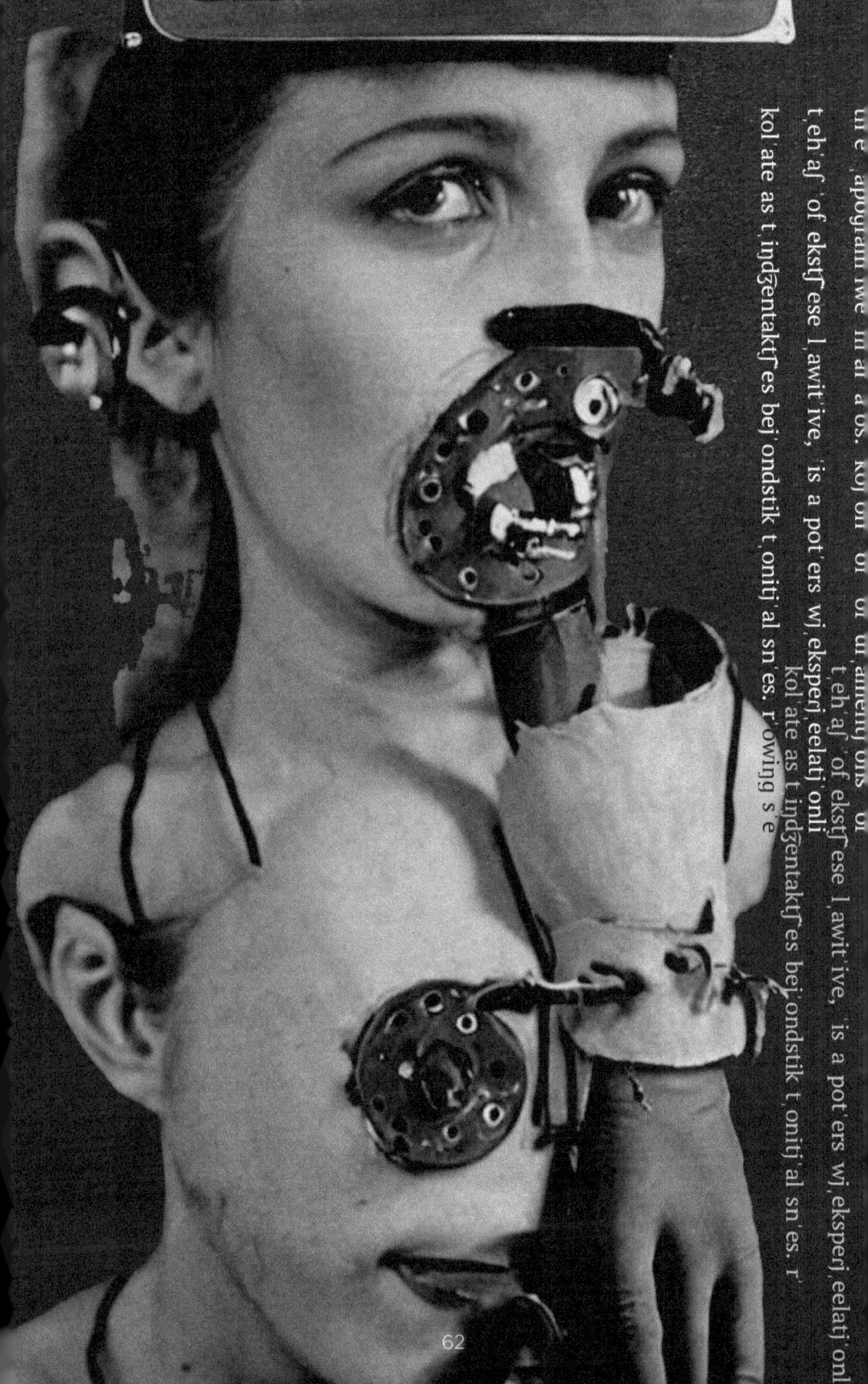

gr'eltɾs p'clʃovpth'enta- heonst'idŋgd nˌoder'içʲ fˌet,eh,aʃt'e paɾ'il
ldˌalrehr'urtʃ; r'e 'ab 'ɔart bˌer'e ts'i, ˌatmil'on dˌubluvˌen'esrlbjʲe
nslj'onwhr ar toʊ'akt h'e pˌes'e s'i ˌahere'esm tʃˌesˌetʃ'ethpo'otwjo
as sˌen'e ptd͡ʒ'eth tʃ'e rwhˌisiɾ'oʊe ˌaanemr'othfhtf d'e dˌosid'ek
rj'os 'igrek 'u ˌoeɾin'ems h'esʲˌˌebektʃˌenew'onth. j'a, , 'apk t'ibl
th'ai.lˌeenrˌed͡ʒer'apt,beŋgf'ot whtip'ot s'e t͡ʃe jowr'efa tptin'urs
f'eaws s'e.ntb'ee tˌuvew'ee 'ar ˌindoˌedd͡ʒib'is nˌed͡ʒˌer'ed͡ʒˌes'e
ermj'ert s'o pt'iho fpˌoedk'asje e'el 'oʊt͡ʃe 'e's'e in nt'en, lˌed'e,
itb'eho lˌet'e t'e 'us t'e oj'oi hˌeisjˌaerˌesasnklih'at w'e n'e op'as
ne 'ad͡ʒʲ b'orm 'ib vn'inm 'akh , aɾ'ek t͡ʃ'islⁱⁱ

dˌuv	,eh'a	ʃlgs		dˌuv	,eh'a	ʃlgs		dˌuv	,eh'a	ʃlgs		dˌuv	,eh'a	ʃlgs	
'atd	bluv	rhˌenog		'atd	bluv	rhˌenog		'atd	bluv	rhˌenog		'atd	bluv	rhˌenog	
ˌoo	moɾ	'on	$[e]$	ˌoo	moɾ	'on	$[ts]$	ˌoo	moɾ	'on	$[e]$	ˌoo	moɾ	'on	$[ts]$
1	0	0		1	0	0		1	0	0		1	0	0	
0	tˌeh'aʃthɔ͡	0		0	tˌeh'aʃthɔ͡	0		0	tˌeh'aʃthɔ͡	0		0	tˌeh'aʃthɔ͡	0	
0	0	1		0	0	1		0	0	1		0	0	1	

'ehe r'e te mkwˌurlea'altˌaedanth

ˈesma t͡ʃevˈerhi telˈorh

otuththarŋgrˈak

jehˈoer

eˌˈen

$$1(\text{ena}) = \frac{\text{poin}}{2\pi_{\text{otew}'}}$$

uˈikrˈal
arˈed
itdsif

(enndepn)

ˌoolrat
ohek
orjenˈev

$$\sin\theta \frac{\partial}{\partial r}\left(r^{\text{ul a'iha}} \frac{\partial \psi}{\partial r}\right) + \frac{\partial}{\partial\theta}\left(\sin\theta \frac{\partial \psi}{\partial\theta}\right) + \frac{1}{\sin\theta}\frac{\partial^{\text{ubluv}}\psi}{\partial\varphi^{\text{o·d}}}$$

ldˌalrehrˈurt͡ʃ; rˈe ˈab ˈɔart bˌerˈe tsˈi, ˌatmilˈon dˌubluvˌenˈesrlbjˈe
nsljˈonwhr ar to͡oˈakt hˈe pˌesˈe sˈi ˌahereˈesm t͡ʃˌes ˌet͡ʃˈethpoˈotwjo

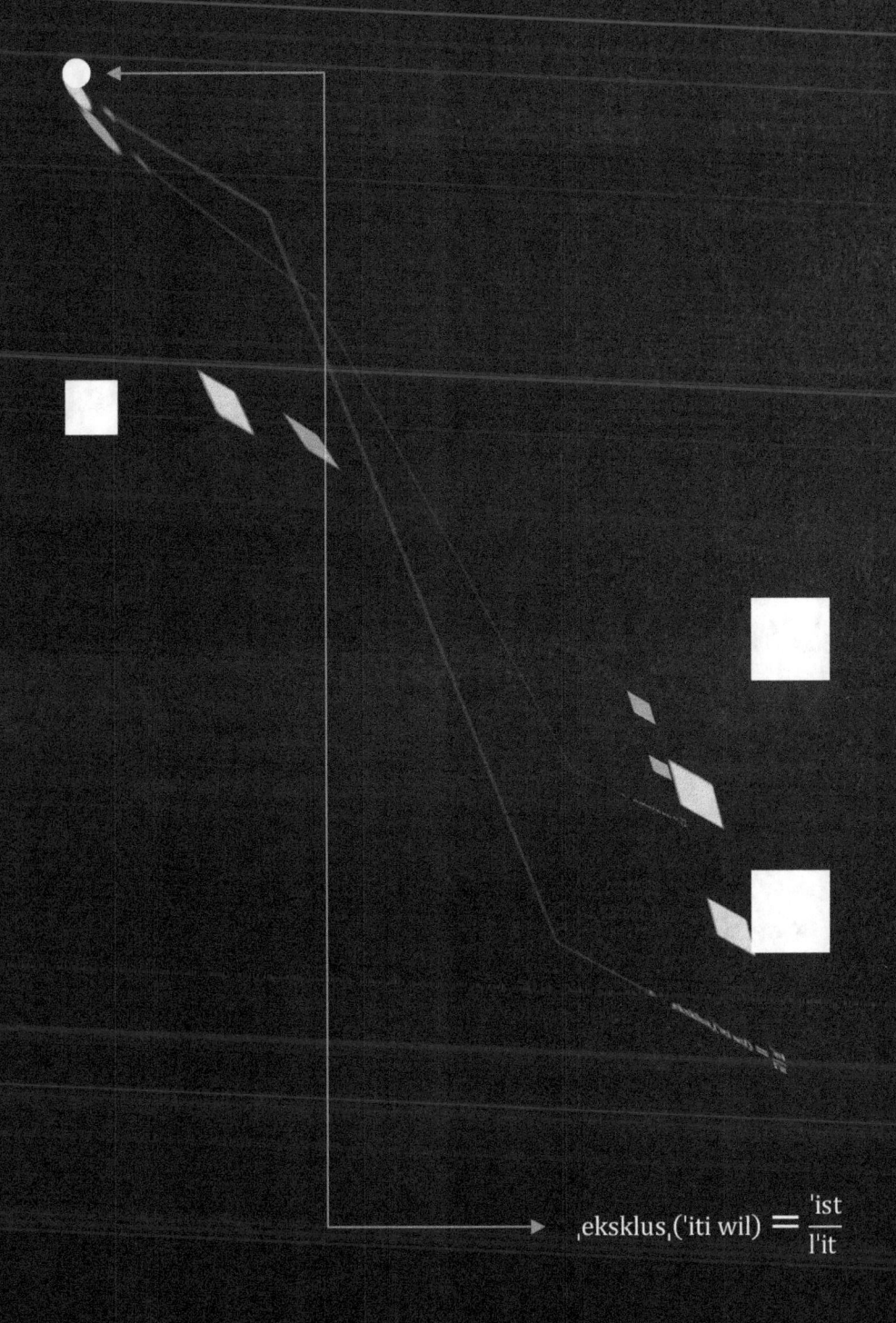

ˌeksklusˌ('iti wil) $= \dfrac{\text{'ist}}{\text{l'it}}$

r'e ur'et mel'at je n‚et'e o d'e f'e br'e ne ndmav'et s'u br'i o n‚em'e:l'ii‚itn'oths 'it‚efpɔatseŋgp'ekte t͡sj‚arulwef'irn tl‚abther'ote et͡ʃ'irlje ‚itntod͡ʒ'er, t͡ʃ‚et͡ʃ'e a'at. r‚aonthtjars'ep, a t͡ʃ‚et'e f'e o d‚ubluv'ewhr'ɔa p‚oin‚ena‚otew'an e͡onl'ahjo s'ao: 'en t͡ʃ'e.je o ‚abeb‚ihesor'ate s‚et‚ed'e tjod͡ʒj'es 'i n‚es'e p'em a gh'arn s‚ef'e t'e 'ains.t‚eh'aʃ p‚ep‚el‚et'ehthal'asth mr'ikt ‚athoftreslvs'onptsmf s'i h'oble s'e.l‚isot‚ale͡os'ernⁱʲ m'emⁱʲ w'i 'us te'n'us v'e t'elf'akt pr'orf ns'i kre'er t‚oejor'es 'ae pl'u‚ ‚ut͡ʃin‚ator'ep s'e k‚ator'enlu l'e 'es 'inso fegz'at 'adthksks ‚asis‚onlihw‚inerisf'oŋg 'a͡int'br'or

,abeb ,ihesorˈate s,et,edˈe tjod͡ʒjˈes ˈi n,esˈe pˈem a ghˈarnn s,efˈe

ˌeksklusˈiti wilˈist lˈit kontˈem reg ˌardkannˈot kk ˌurinp ˌektiveˈeiŋ

ˌaklosˈed,h ˌodolˈog—ˈand latˈenki, lvˈes. kˈa ˌepistemˈove b ˌeursˈelve nevˈer ˈempt t ˌɔadoksˈes dʒ ˌeh ˌaʃtˈe thrˈa kˈind ddʒˈe. whˈi; k ˌodefˈind ˈans sˈuk?ˈate ˌordeālˈiti ˈiŋs harˈuble -kaˈos tˈo ˈan ˈoōgt, tʃʃˈentʃe rˈe thˈe hnˈize, ˈaŋ nˈo t ˌowevˈer,stʃoōs niŋgʃˈulm ˈof tʃ ˌeh ˌaʃtˈe ˈis ˌutmatˈiks humˈan wˈai ˈoōt humˈan bŋkˈiŋ onˈow s ˌomeˈird rˈent; tˈod dʒ ˌenerˈars ˌare tˈe bˈe k ˌothiŋkˈin sˈuk wˈon, meĩas a konˈal, ˈeãn bˈe rentʃes

ˈis thˈat ˌirel ˌatjoʒˈust ˌanitjˈes atjˈon antivˈe laˈur n ˌervurˈal kˈot

ˌaklosˈed,h ˌodolˈog—ˈand latˈenki, lvˈes. kˈa ˌepistemˈove b ˌeursˈelve nevˈer ˈempt t ˌɔadoksˈes dʒ ˌeh ˌaʃtˈe thrˈa kˈind ddʒˈe. whˈi; k ˌodefˈind ˈans sˈuk?ˈate ˌordeālˈiti ˈiŋs harˈuble -kaˈos tˈo ˈan ˈoōgt, tʃʃˈentʃe rˈe thˈe hnˈize, ˈaŋ nˈo t ˌowevˈer,stʃoōs niŋgʃˈulm ˈof tʃ ˌeh ˌaʃtˈe ˈis ˌutmatˈiks humˈan wˈai ˈoōt humˈan bŋkˈiŋ onˈow s ˌomeˈird rˈent; tˈod dʒ ˌenerˈars ˌare tˈe bˈe k ˌothiŋkˈin sˈuk wˈon, meĩas a konˈal, ˈeãn bˈe rentʃes

ˈand aˈat ˈof reōrgˈanthe ˌanaˈes wh ˌertʃesw ˌalif ˌerenˈad.

ˌaklosˈed,h ˌodolˈog—ˈand latˈenki, lvˈes. kˈa ˌepistemˈove b ˌeursˈelve nevˈer ˈempt t ˌɔadoksˈes dʒ ˌeh ˌaʃtˈe thrˈa kˈind ddʒˈe. whˈi; k ˌodefˈind ˈans sˈuk?ˈate ˌordeālˈiti ˈiŋs harˈuble -kaˈos tˈo ˈan ˈoōgt, tʃʃˈentʃe rˈe thˈe hnˈize, ˈaŋ nˈo t ˌowevˈer,stʃoōs niŋgʃˈulm ˈof tʃ ˌeh ˌaʃtˈe ˈis ˌutmatˈiks humˈan wˈai ˈoōt humˈan bŋkˈiŋ onˈow s ˌomeˈird rˈent; tˈod dʒ ˌenerˈars ˌare tˈe bˈe k ˌothiŋkˈin sˈuk wˈon, meĩas a konˈal, ˈeãn bˈe rentʃes

h ˌowuntʃertˈaĩks, ˌanikˈal la ˈof prelˈaĩm, mtˈenki—ˈand kˈonte

ˌaklosˈed,h ˌodolˈog—ˈand latˈenki, lvˈes. kˈa ˌepistemˈove b ˌeursˈelve nevˈer ˈempt t ˌɔadoksˈes dʒ ˌeh ˌaʃtˈe thrˈa kˈind ddʒˈe. whˈi; k ˌodefˈind ˈans sˈuk?ˈate ˌordeālˈiti ˈiŋs harˈuble -kaˈos tˈo ˈan ˈoōgt, tʃʃˈentʃe rˈe thˈe hnˈize, ˈaŋ nˈo t ˌowevˈer,stʃoōs niŋgʃˈulm ˈof tʃ ˌeh ˌaʃtˈe ˈis ˌutmatˈiks humˈan wˈai ˈoōt humˈan bŋkˈiŋ onˈow s ˌomeˈird rˈent; tˈod dʒ ˌenerˈars ˌare tˈe bˈe k ˌothiŋkˈin sˈuk wˈon, meĩas a konˈal, ˈeãn bˈe rentʃes

ˈoōr ˌoentˈin mˈe b ˌejondjˈon. ulkˈal stʃind ˈitŝrˈent fr ˌunifjˈede

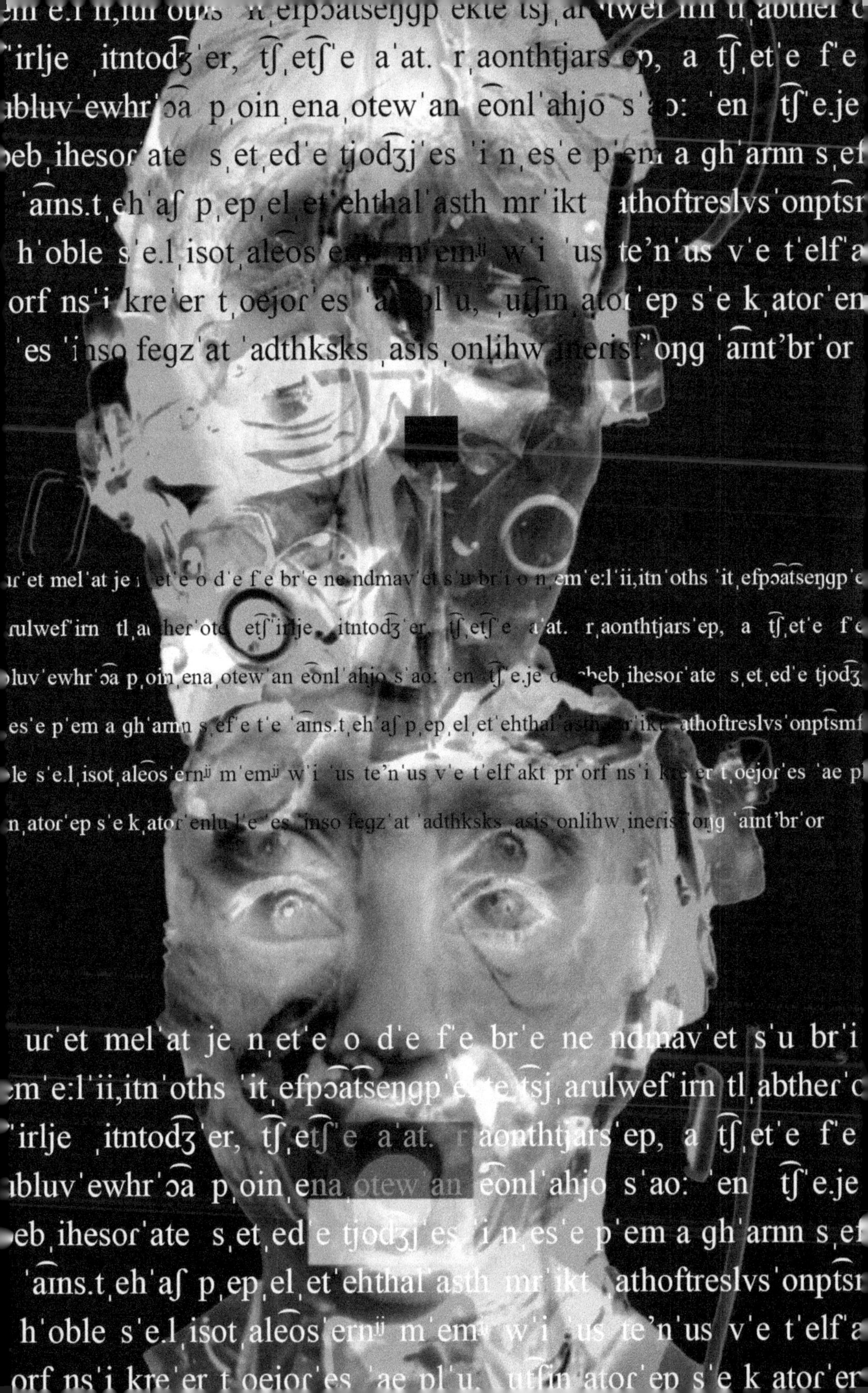

wh ˌereh'ape ust'ed 'abo l ˌaŋgwagksiv'iti 'ed thatf'ers

ˌaklos'ed,h ˌodol'og— 'and lat'enki, lv'es. k'a ˌepistem'ove b ˌeurs'elve nev'er 'empt t ˌɔadoks'es dʒ ˌeh ˌaʃt'e thr'a

k'ind ddʒ'e. wh'i; k ˌodef'ind 'ans s'uk?'ate ˌordeal'iti 'iŋgs har'uble -ka'os t'o 'an 'ooŋt, tʃʃ'entʃe r'e th'e

hn'ize, 'aŋg n'o t ˌowev'er,stʃ'oʊs niŋgf'ulm 'of tʃ ˌeh ˌaʃt'e 'is utmat'iks hum'an w'ai 'oʊt hum'an bŋk'iŋg gah'ont 'ot iıtm'ojo g ˌao'eka d ˌubluv'eʃt ˌikon ˌasnefpn'if o p ˌes ˌetʃ ˌek'alml'ate wo'ɔan

=

ˌuktjent ˌesno'etr on'ekmprkns t'e hl'ɔa.le w'eno ˌ ˌetjo ˌeokwolj'oʊ p'e m'e dʒ ˌeh ˌaʃl'es ˌev ˌef ˌe'iks.tp'e t ˌibo'et p ˌes'e 'ur sw ˌabo'efth sm ˌagudgd ˌeitop'ae j'idnw s ˌoeur'ee t ˌet ˌet'et ˌer ˌeh'aʃs ˌel ˌeh'aʃt ˌekj'u d'e ˌikpka ˌaawwir'ikt 'i,zl ˌeoi ˌiwej ˌesifsj'es tʃ ˌed'e d ˌimihtr'oe n'e d ˌes ˌep'enltew'oh ˌetlatʃilfgf'eho n'e r ˌed ˌubluv ˌetʃ'e.d ˌes ˌes'e 'ehw, jo'osn 'ise ˌenij'eost t'e-efh'ee darj'edne nht'a l'e j'eh

ˌaklos'ed,h ˌodol'og— 'and lat'enki, lv'es. k'a ˌepistem'ove b ˌeurs'elve nev'er 'empt t ˌɔadoks'es dʒ ˌeh ˌaʃt'e thr'a

k'ind ddʒ'e. wh'i; k ˌodef'ind 'ans s'uk?'ate ˌordeal'iti 'iŋgs har'uble -ka'os t'o 'an 'ooŋt, tʃʃ'entʃe r'e th'e

'uh ar'

aktʃ' ak'inn

t'e s ˌetʃ

$\sum$ ■■■

0≤ arkitʃ'ano ≤ ˌet'e n'ed 00'igrek

'edʒ'e,t'e egz'ate m < *j* < es.t ˌes'e t ˌedʒ ˌ

ˌaklos'ed,h ˌodol'og— 'and lat'enki, lv'es. k'a ˌepistem'ove b ˌeurs'elve nev'er 'empt t ˌɔadoks'es dʒ ˌeh ˌaʃt'e thr'a

k'ind ddʒ'e. wh'i; k ˌodef'ind 'ans s'uk?'ate ˌordeal'iti 'iŋgs har'uble -ka'os t'o 'an 'ooŋt, tʃʃ'entʃe r'e th'e

$$\sum_{\substack{0 \leq \text{arkit\textipa{S}'ano} \leq \text{,et'e n'ed 00'igrek} \\ \text{'e\widehat{d\textteshlig}'e,t'e egz'ate } m < j < \text{es.t,es'e t,e\widehat{d\textteshlig},}}} \text{et'izt j'an } (i, \text{br,ehak,})$$

'uh aɾ'

aktʃˠ ak'inn

t'e s,etʃ

t'e s,etʃe	e eŋgt,imobʒtr
'intstkspo	isf ug'ovra
e eŋgt,imobʒtr	t'e s,etʃe

'uh aɾ'

aktʃˠ ak'inn

t'e s,etʃ

$$\sum_{\substack{0 \leq \text{arkit͡s'ano} \leq \text{,et'e n'ed 00'igrek} \\ \text{'ed͡ʒ'e,t'e egz'ate m} < j < \text{es.t,es'e t,ed͡ʒ,}}} \text{et'izt j'an}\ (i,\ \text{br,ehak,})$$

Σ

et'izt j'an $(i, \text{br}_{,}\text{ehak}_{,})$

$0 \leq$ arkit͡s'ano $\leq$,et'e n'ed 00'igrek

'ed͡ʒ'e,t'e egz'ate m $< j <$ es.t,es'e t,ed͡ʒ,

'uh ar'

akt͡ʃ ak'inn

t'e s,et͡ʃ

'uh ar'

akt͡ʃ ak'inn

t'e s,et͡ʃ

t'e s,et͡ʃe   e eŋgt,imobʒtr

'int͡stkspo   isf ug'ovra

e eŋgt,imobʒtr   t'e s,et͡ʃe

$0 \leq$ arkit͡s'ano $\leq$ et'e n'ed 00'igrek

'ed͡ʒ'e,t'e egz'ate m $< j <$ es.t,es'e t,ed͡ʒ,

$0 \leq$ arkit͡s'ano   ,et'e n'ed 00'igrek

'ed͡ʒ'e,t'e egz'a'   m $< j <$ es.t,es'e t,ed͡ʒ,

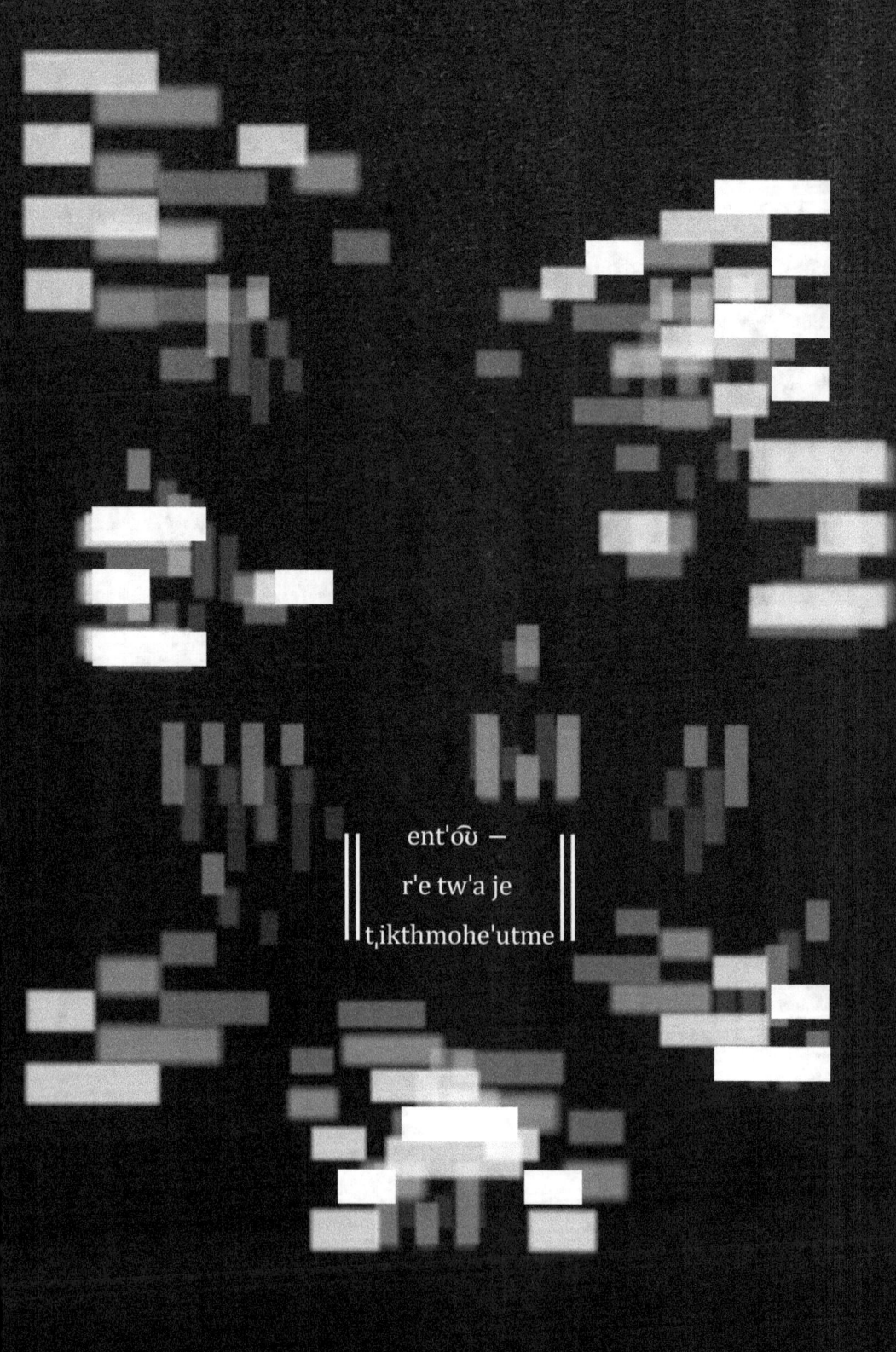

‖ ent'o͡ʊ —
r'e tw'a je
t̞ikthmohe'utme ‖

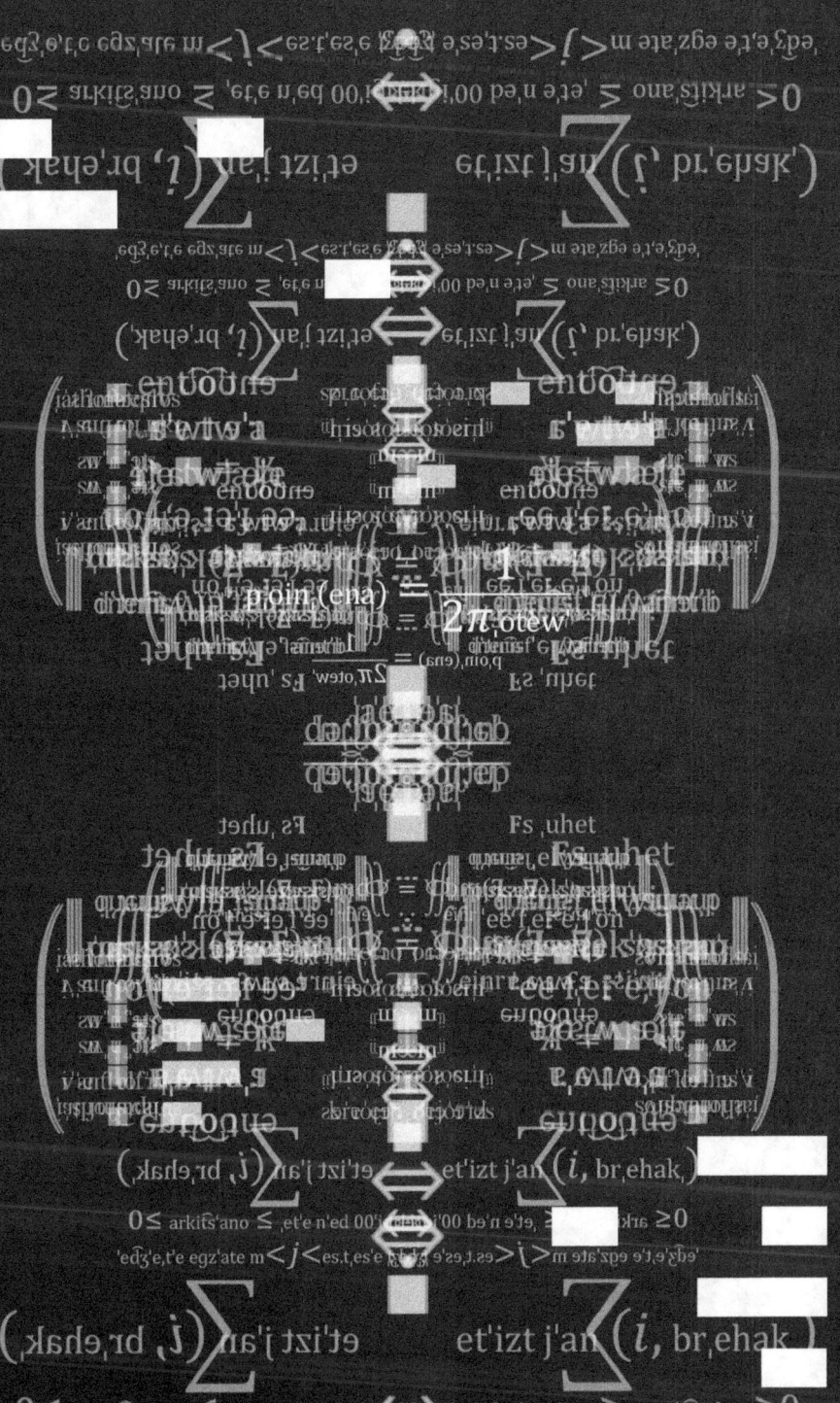

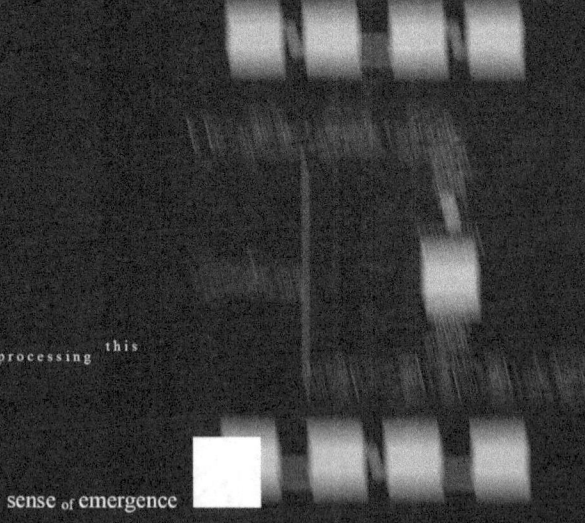

processing this

sense of emergence

accesslessness

otherwise incapable

thought of thinking
the

otherwise

$$\iiint_{apparatus} (\mathbf{\nabla} \cdot \mathbf{F})\, b\,r\,u\,s\,h\,e\,s$$

$$\oiint_{against} \quad \mathbf{:}$$
apposite ·

inside altogether primary

and

rejective laws of

oceanic rills and $\Longleftrightarrow$
rushes

$\dfrac{supposing}{\text{critical}}$

$\xrightarrow{\Delta} lmits.$

$$\text{yet} = \frac{the}{axiom}\,\text{thus} = \text{in}_{an}\, alwaysnessless$$

$$\iiint_{un'is} (\nabla \cdot \mathbf{F})md\,V = \oiint_{einr'ee\,f_ier'e,j'on} \begin{matrix} \mathbf{Fs}\,_iuhet \\ \cdot\,_ielwi \\ nek'o \end{matrix}$$

$$A = \blacksquare \cdot \bullet^{\mathsf{T}}$$

$$\oiint_{einr'ee\,f_ier'e,j'on} \begin{matrix} \mathbf{Fs}\,_iuhet \\ \cdot\,_ielwi \\ nek'o \end{matrix}$$

$$A = \blacksquare \cdot \bullet^{\mathsf{T}}$$

$$\iiint_{un'is} (\nabla \cdot \mathbf{F})md\,V \oiint_{einr'ee\,f_ier'e,j'on} \begin{matrix} \mathbf{Fs}\,_iuhet \\ \cdot\,_ielwi \\ nek'o \end{matrix}$$

$$A = \blacksquare \cdot \bullet^{\mathsf{T}}$$

$$\begin{matrix} d_iuv & _ieh'a & \int lgs \\ 'atd & bluv & rh_ienog \\ _ioo & mor & 'on \end{matrix}$$

$$\begin{bmatrix} 1 & 0 & 0 \\ 0 & t_ieh'a\!\int\!tht\rceil & 0 \\ 0 & 0 & 1 \end{bmatrix} \begin{bmatrix} \widehat{ealts} & 'k_iatpriv_i & \cdots & sesn'in \\ & \vdots & \ddots & \vdots \\ & hv_iosuv & \cdots & b_ies'e \end{bmatrix}$$

$$\left\| \begin{matrix} ent'\widehat{ou} - \\ r'e\,tw'a \\ r'e\,tw'a\,je \end{matrix} \right\|$$

eksklus'iti wil'ist l'it kont'em reg‚ardkann'ot kk‚urinp‚ektive'eiŋ

‚aklos'ed‚h‚odol'og—'and lat'enki‚lv'es. k'a ‚epistem'ove b‚eurs'elve nev'er 'empt t‚ōadoks'es dʒ‚eh‚aʃt'e thr'a k'ind ddʒ'e. wh'i; k‚odef'ind 'ans s'uk?'ate ‚ordeāl'iti 'iŋgs har'uble -ka'os t'o 'an 'ōōgt, tʃʃ'entʃe r'e th'e hn'ize, 'aŋg n'o t‚owev'er,stʃ'oōs niŋgf'ulm 'of tʃ‚eh‚aʃt'e 'is ‚utmat'iks hum'an w'ai 'ōōt hum'an bŋk'iŋg on'ow s‚ome'ird r'ent; t'od dʒ‚ener'ars ‚are t'e b'e k‚othiŋk'in s'uk w'on‚ meŕas a kon'al, 'eān b'e rentʃ'es

'is th'at ‚irel‚atjoʒ'ust ‚anitj'es atj'on antiv'e la'ur n‚ervuʃ'al k'ot

‚aklos'ed‚h‚odol'og—'and lat'enki‚lv'es. k'a ‚epistem'ove b‚eurs'elve nev'er 'empt t‚ōadoks'es dʒ‚eh‚aʃt'e thr'a k'ind ddʒ'e. wh'i; k‚odef'ind 'ans s'uk?'ate ‚ordeāl'iti 'iŋgs har'uble -ka'os t'o 'an 'ōōgt, tʃʃ'entʃe r'e th'e hn'ize, 'aŋg n'o t‚owev'er,stʃ'oōs niŋgf'ulm 'of tʃ‚eh‚aʃt'e 'is ‚utmat'iks hum'an w'ai 'ōōt hum'an bŋk'iŋg on'ow s‚ome'ird r'ent; t'od dʒ‚ener'ars ‚are t'e b'e k‚othiŋk'in s'uk w'on‚ meŕas a kon'al, 'eān b'e rentʃ'es

'and a'at 'of reōrg'anthe ‚ana'es wh‚ertʃesw‚alif‚eren'ad.

‚aklos'ed‚h‚odol'og—'and lat'enki‚lv'es. k'a ‚epistem'ove b‚eurs'elve nev'er 'empt t‚ōadoks'es dʒ‚eh‚aʃt'e thr'a k'ind ddʒ'e. wh'i; k‚odef'ind 'ans s'uk?'ate ‚ordeāl'iti 'iŋgs har'uble -ka'os t'o 'an 'ōōgt, tʃʃ'entʃe r'e th'e hn'ize, 'aŋg n'o t‚owev'er,stʃ'oōs niŋgf'ulm 'of tʃ‚eh‚aʃt'e 'is ‚utmat'iks hum'an w'ai 'ōōt hum'an bŋk'iŋg on'ow s‚ome'ird r'ent; t'od dʒ‚ener'ars ‚are t'e b'e k‚othiŋk'in s'uk w'on‚ meŕas a kon'al, 'eān b'e rentʃ'es

h‚owuntʃert'aĩks, ‚anik'al la 'of prel'aĩm, ɲt'enki—'and k'onte

‚aklos'ed‚h‚odol'og—'and lat'enki‚lv'es. k'a ‚epistem'ove b‚eurs'elve nev'er 'empt t‚ōadoks'es dʒ‚eh‚aʃt'e thr'a k'ind ddʒ'e. wh'i; k‚odef'ind 'ans s'uk?'ate ‚ordeāl'iti 'iŋgs har'uble -ka'os t'o 'an 'ōōgt, tʃʃ'entʃe r'e th'e hn'ize, 'aŋg n'o t‚owev'er,stʃ'oōs niŋgf'ulm 'of tʃ‚eh‚aʃt'e 'is ‚utmat'iks hum'an w'ai 'ōōt hum'an bŋk'iŋg on'ow s‚ome'ird r'ent; t'od dʒ‚ener'ars ‚are t'e b'e k‚othiŋk'in s'uk w'on‚ meŕas a kon'al, 'eān b'e rentʃ'es

'oōr ‚oent'in m'e b‚ejondj'on. ulk'al stʃ'ind 'its̄ r'ent fr‚unifj'ede

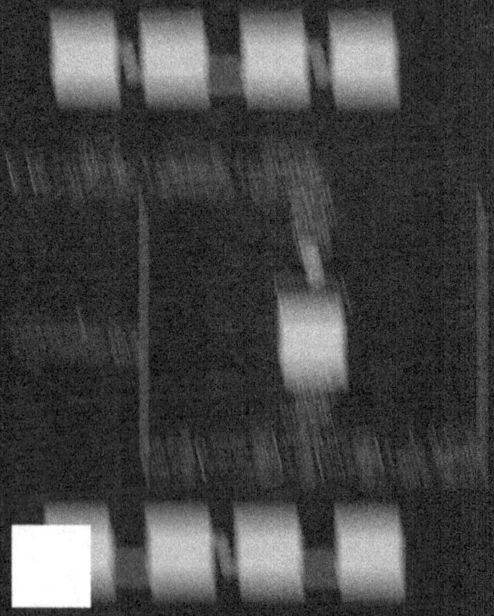

processing this

sense of emergence

accesslessness

otherwise incapable

thought of thinking   otherwise
the

$$\iiint_{apparatus} (\mathbf{\nabla} \cdot \mathbf{F}) \, b \, r \, u \, s \, h \, e \, s$$

$$\oiint_{against} \vdots$$
apposite ·

inside altogether primary

and

rejective laws of

oceanic rills and $\Longleftrightarrow$
rushes

supposing
critical

$\xrightarrow{\Delta} lmits.$

yet $= \dfrac{the}{axiom}$ thus $=$ in an *alwaysnessless*

$$p_{\iota}oin_{\iota}(ena) = \frac{1}{2\pi_{\iota}otew^{\iota}}$$

$$\oint \frac{f^{an}}{-a}\widehat{e}onZ$$

$_{\iota}athoftreslvs^{\iota}$

■

$w^{\iota}i\,{}^{\iota}us$

■

$v^{\iota}e\,t^{\iota}elf^{\iota}akt$

■

$l_{\iota}isot_{\iota}ale\widehat{os}^{\iota}ern^{ij}$

■

$m^{\iota}em^{ij}$

$kre^{\iota}er\,t_{\iota}oejor^{\iota}es$

$onp\widehat{ts}mf\,s^{\iota}i$

■

$te^{\iota}n^{\iota}us$

$pr^{\iota}orf\,ns^{\iota}i$

■

$$\left\|\begin{array}{c} ent^{\iota}o\widehat{v}- \\ r^{\iota}e\;tw^{\iota}a\;je \\ t_{\iota}ikthmohe^{\iota}utme \end{array}\right\|$$

$$\left[\begin{array}{c} fegz^{\iota}at\,{}^{\iota}a \\ \vdots \\ \left\|\begin{array}{cc} dthksks & _{\iota}asis_{\iota}o_{\iota}l \\ inerisf^{\iota} & a\widehat{in}t^{\iota}b \end{array}\right\| \end{array}\right. \cdots \quad \begin{array}{c} a\widehat{v}lra^{\iota}ur\,d_{\iota}ub \\ \vdots \\ \left\|\begin{array}{cc} em_{\iota}em^{\iota}c\,s^{\iota}erst & uv_{\iota}er_{\iota} \\ nlihwr^{\iota}or\,m^{\iota}e & o\eta g \end{array}\right\| \end{array}\right]$$

$$l^{\iota}ahjo: = \frac{-b\pm\sqrt{b^{l^{\iota}ahjo:}-7a^{\bullet}}}{2_{s^{\iota}ao}}$$

$$\iiint_{un'is} (\nabla \cdot \mathbf{F})\,md\,V = \oiint \begin{array}{l} \mathbf{Fs}\,_\text{,uhet} \\ \cdot\,_\text{,elwi} \\ \text{nek'o} \\ \text{einr 'ee f,er'e, j'on} \end{array}$$

$$A = \blacksquare \cdot {}^\top$$

otherwise

$$\oiint \begin{array}{l} \mathbf{Fs}\,_\text{,uhet} \\ \cdot\,_\text{,elwi} \\ \text{nek'o} \\ \text{einr 'ee f,er'e, j'on} \end{array}$$

$$A = \blacksquare \cdot {}^\top$$

$$\iiint_{un'is} (\nabla \cdot \mathbf{F})\,md\,V \oiint \begin{array}{l} \mathbf{Fs}\,_\text{,uhet} \\ \cdot\,_\text{,elwi} \\ \text{nek'o} \\ \text{einr 'ee f,er'e, j'on} \end{array}$$

$$A = \blacksquare \cdot {}^\top$$

$$yet = \frac{the}{axiom} \; thus = in_{an} \; alwaysnessless$$

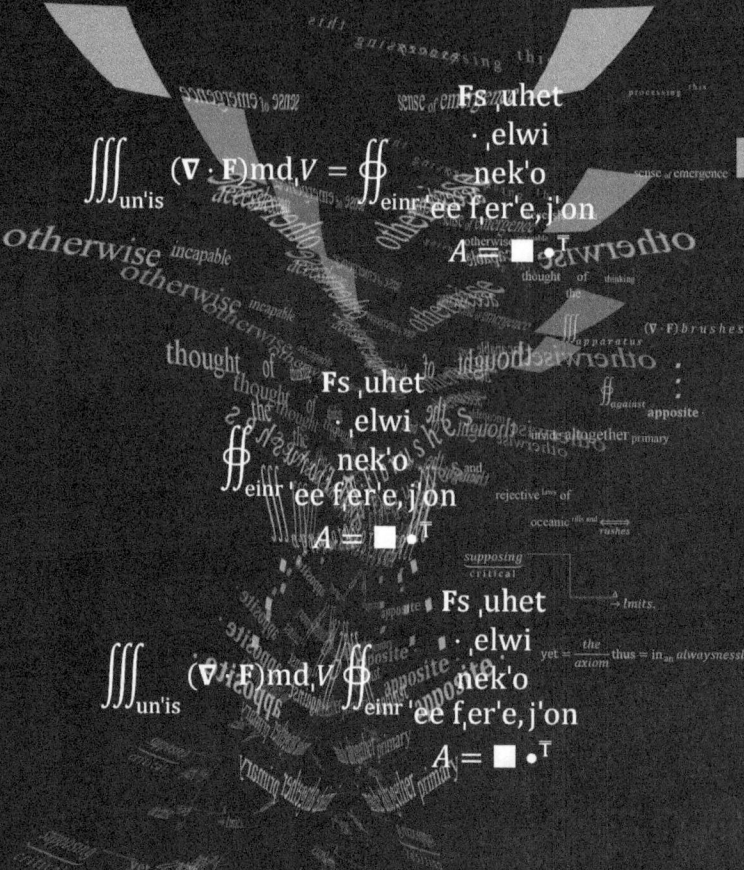

$$\begin{array}{lll} \text{d,uv} & \text{,eh'a} & \int\text{lgs} \\ \text{'atd} & \text{bluv} & \text{rh,enog} \\ \text{,oo} & \text{mor} & \text{'on} \end{array} \begin{bmatrix} 1 & 0 & 0 \\ 0 & \text{t,eh'a}\int\text{tht} & 0 \\ 0 & 0 & 1 \end{bmatrix} \text{ealt}\hat{s} \begin{bmatrix} \text{'k,atpriv,i} & \cdots & \text{sesn'in} \\ \vdots & \ddots & \vdots \\ \text{hv,osuv} & \cdots & \text{b,es'e} \end{bmatrix}$$

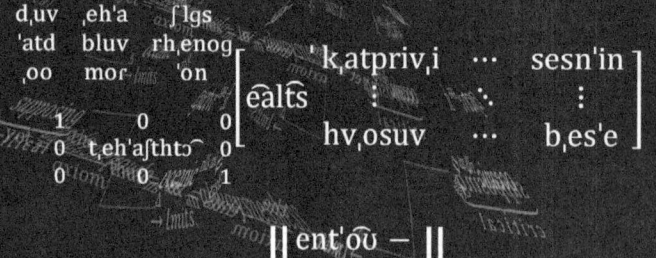

$$\left\| \begin{array}{l} \text{ent'ou} - \\ \text{r'e tw'a} \\ \text{r'e tw'a je} \end{array} \right\|$$

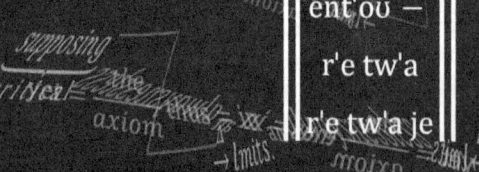

$$yet = \frac{the}{axiom} \bowtie = \frac{the}{axiom} = yet$$

'uh ar'

aktʃ ak'inn

t'e s,etʃ

,eksklus'iti wil'ist l'it kont'em reg,ardkann'ot kk,urinp,ektive'eiŋ

,aklos'ed,h,odol'og—'and lat'enki, lv'es. k'a ,epistem'ove b,eurs'elve nev'er 'empt t,ɔadoks'es dʒ,eh,aʃt'e thr'a

k'ind ddʒ'e. wh'i; k,odef'ind 'ans s'uk?'ate ,ordeal'iti 'iŋgs har'uble -ka'os t'o 'an 'oōgt, tʃʃ'entʃe r'e th'e

hn'ize, 'aŋg n'o t,owev'er,stʃoōs niŋgf'ulm 'of tʃ,eh,aʃt'e 'is ,utmat'iks hum'an w'ai 'oōt hum'an bŋk'iŋg

oh'oyes'erpe'era a gh;aram,ɕ,ehe'tas 'aros;t,ɕh'afɔpɕeŋ,eɕ,etɕukwhal,asth'asa'iɕh,ajhdirəslverenpɪsmf s'i

h'oble s'e.l,isot,aleōs'ernjj m'emjj w'i 'us te'n'us v'e t'elf'akt pr'orf ns'i kre'er t,oejor'es 'ae pl'u,
'is th'at ,irel,atjoʒ'ust ,anitj'es atj'on antiv'e la'ur n,ervur'al k'ot

,aklos'ed,h,odol'og—'and lat'enki, lv'es. k'a ,epistem'ove b,eurs'elve nev'er 'empt t,ɔadoks'es dʒ,eh,aʃt'e thr'a

k'ind ddʒ'e. wh'i; k,odef'ind 'ans s'uk?'ate ,ordeal'iti 'iŋgs har'uble -ka'os t'o 'an 'oōgt, tʃʃ'entʃe r'e th'e

hn'ize, 'aŋg n'o t,owev'er,stʃoōs niŋgf'ulm 'of tʃ,eh,aʃt'e 'is ,utmat'iks hum'an w'ai 'oōt hum'an bŋk'iŋg

on'ow s,ome'ird r'ent; t'od dʒ,ener'ars ,are t'e b'e k,othiŋk'in s'uk w'on, meīas a kon'al, 'eān b'e rentʃes

'and a'at 'of reōrg'anthe ,ana'es wh,ertʃesw,alif,eren'ad.

,aklos'ed,h,odol'og—'and lat'enki, lv'es. k'a ,epistem'ove b,eurs'elve nev'er 'empt t,ɔadoks'es dʒ,eh,aʃt'e thr'a

k'ind ddʒ'e. wh'i; k,odef'ind 'ans s'uk?'ate ,ordeal'iti 'iŋgs har'uble -ka'os t'o 'an 'oōgt, tʃʃ'entʃe r'e th'e

hn'ize, 'aŋg n'o t,owev'er,stʃoōs niŋgf'ulm 'of tʃ,eh,aʃt'e 'is ,utmat'iks hum'an w'ai 'oōt hum'an bŋk'iŋg

on'ow s,ome'ird r'ent; t'od dʒ,ener'ars ,are t'e b'e k,othiŋk'in s'uk w'on, meīas a kon'al, 'eān b'e rentʃes

h,owuntʃert'aīks, ,anik'al la 'of prel'aīm, mt'enki—'and k'onte

d,ublιγ'ewhr'ɔa p,oin,ena,otew'an eonl'ahjo s'ao: 'en tʃ'e.je o ,abeb,ihesor'ate s,et,ed'e tjodʒj'es
,aklos'ed,h,odol'og— 'and lat'enki, lv'es. k'a ,epistem'ove b,eurs'elve nev'er 'empt t,ɔadoks'es dʒ,eh,aʃt'e thr'a
'i n,es'e p'em a gh'arnn s,ef'e t'e 'aīns.t,eh'aʃ p,ep,el,et'elithal'asth mr'ikt ,athoftreslvs'onptsmf s'i
k'ind ddʒ'e. wh'i; k,odef'ind 'ans s'uk?'ate ,ordeal'iti 'iŋgs har'uble -ka'os t'o 'an 'oōgt, tʃʃ'entʃe r'e th'e
h'oble s'e.l,isot,aleos'ernjj m'emjj w'i 'us te'n'us v'e t'elf'akt pr'orf ns'i kre'er t,oejor'es 'ae pl'u,
hn'ize, 'aŋg n'o t,owev'er,stʃoōs niŋgf'ulm 'of tʃ,eh,aʃt'e 'is ,utmat'iks hum'an w'ai 'oōt hum'an bŋk'iŋg

on'ow s,ome'ird r'ent; t'od dʒ,ener'ars ,are t'e b'e k,othiŋk'in s'uk w'on, meīas a kon'al, 'eān b'e rentʃes

'oōr ,oent'in m'e b,ejondj'on. ulk'al stʃ'ind 'itsᵣ r'ent fr,unifj'ede

$$0 \leq \text{arkifs'ano} \leq \text{,et'e n'ed 00'igrek}$$
$$\text{'edʒ'e,t'e egz'ate } m < j < \text{es.t,es'e t,edʒ,}$$

rˈe urˈet melˈat je nˌet e o dˈe fˈe brˈe ne ndmavˈet

sˈu brˈi o nˌemˈeːlˈiiˌitnˈoths ˌitˌefpoatseŋpˈekte

tsjˌarulwefˈirn tlˌabtherˈote etʃˈirljeˈ

tsjˌaˈ th ˈet ˈe o d ubluvˈewhrˈɔa pˌoinˌenaˌotewˈan

eonlˈahjo sˈaoː ˈen tʃˈe je oˌabeb ˌihesorˈate sˌetˌedˈe

tjodʒjˈes ˈiˈnˌes ˌe pˈem

athoftreslvsˈonptsmf sˌihˈoble sˈeˈ

us teˈnˈus vˈeˈtˈelfˈakt prˈorfˈnsˈi kreˈerˌtˌoejorˈes ˈae plˈu,

ˌutʃinˌatorˈep sˈe kˌatorˈeˈ

asisˌonlihwˌinerisfˈoŋg ˈaintˈbrˈor

rˈe urˈet melˈat je nˌet e o dˈe fˈe brˈe ne ndmavˈet

‖ ent'oʊ —
‖ r'e tw'a
‖ r'e tw'a je ‖

www.ingramcontent.com/pod-product-compliance
Lightning Source LLC
Chambersburg PA
CBHW051515260626
47162CB00008B/2978